RECOMPENSE

By

HOWARD LYCETT

THANKS

Once again, I must give thanks to a number of people who have given up their free time in helping me produce my fourth book.

Padraig Sweeney, my loyal researcher, who was a little caught out having to research the other side of the peace wall. I'm sure your mate Gerry will forgive you this time.

Lou Shelley, my fantastic proof-reader, even though the brutality of the stories shocks her. She does a fantastic job in making my gibberish readable.

Paul Martin, my cover designer, who brings my mad ideas to life and produces some very eye-catching designs. Not only is he a great rugby player but a top bloke.

My Mum, Patricia Lycett, for buying my books - and her friends for kindly reading her "Presents."

To Paul from Tesco's in Leigh thanks for helping those two reprobates with their shopping every Friday, but they are using you as a distraction while they are shop lifting!

My ever-suffering wife, Janet, for trying to look interested when I try and describe a storyline to her. Your new bungalow will soon be affordable!

Lastly my steadily growing band of loyal readers: thanks for your feedback and interaction. Enjoy the new adventure.

This book is dedicated to all the brave men and women I have served with for twenty-two years since leaving the military, fighting crime, and appeasing the masses.

Hamstrung by the laws they are trying to uphold.

Overworked, underpaid, under constant strain and scrutiny.

I have laughed with them and cried with them.

Shared their frustrations and successes.

May your shifts be safe, and your arrests be successful.

In Remembrance of PC Stephen Oake QPM, Nicola Hughes, and Fiona Bone. Fine, brave officers who paid the ultimate price doing a job they loved.

IN THE LINE OF DUTY

FOREWARD

A thought came to me on a wet windy afternoon as I stood outside a tiny chapel situated inside a cold graveyard in Eccles, Greater Manchester. I was surrounded by brothers from other mothers. Our only link was that we all wore a red and white hackle in our berets.

I had served with a few; others had been in one of our sister battalions or served on a different timeline for me.

Some of the guys had travelled many miles to pay their respects to the soldier in the coffin.

Mick Healy was a quiet man, softly spoken, but when he did speak it was always worth listening to.

He was a fine warrior and left the battalion too soon. He didn't just leave, he disappeared from the face of the earth. Many of his friends tried to find him, but it's hard to find somebody who does not want to be found.

We didn't know about any family, past or present. In fact, the only snapshot any of us had about Mick's life was his time in the army.

After his demise we found out he lived about five miles away from some of his closest friends, comrades who had served on operations with him, drunk with him and stood shoulder to shoulder and fought beside him.

I realised that I had been out of the mob almost as long as I had been in it. I have worked for the police for nearly twenty-two years. I admire their dedication and note their daily frustrations of being hampered by politicians, do gooders, and the lords of a woke generation.

This novel is dedicated to the brave men and women of the police service, the piggies in the middle (no pun intended) who cannot do right for doing wrong. Like in my previous occupation they step forward into danger, not shying away.

They are like goalkeepers in football: if they make a mistake, they are quickly damned, if they are doing well, they are never acknowledged, but God forbid if they ever left the field.

Just like Corporal Michael Healy, whom we never truly acknowledged, but now miss so much.

Recompense:

Verb: make amends to (someone) for loss or harm suffered; compensate.

INTRODUCTION

Windsor Park, Belfast, October 1998

The black front door of the neatly kept terraced house opened again, allowing two more volunteers to join the group specially selected for the mission. The owners had been given fifty quid and ordered to make themselves scarce for a few hours whilst a political meeting took place.

The saloon car which had dropped them off disappeared into the night.

One by one they had met their contact outside the national football stadium at Windsor Park, then taken on a ten-minute anti-surveillance drive through the backstreets of the Village, a Protestant stronghold which was only separated from the nationalist St James estate by the M1 motorway.

Now they sat patiently in the front room staring at the magnolia walls, with no television or radio to distract them. Locked in their own thoughts about the forthcoming unknown task.

A tall and skinny bald man pulled on his fingers, the guy beside him flinched at every crack. Another kept rubbing his greasy black hair whilst the youngest man looked down at his black work boots.

Rain was drumming violently against the windows.

It had not been a good month for the Protestant paramilitary groups. Infighting between the Ulster Defence Force and Ulster Volunteer Force had caused more deaths than the Provisional Irish Republican Army had ever managed to achieve.

Whilst the factions fought, the Republican dissident groups took their chance by infiltrating the Loyalist estates, planting under-car booby traps on off-duty police officers' vehicles and assassinating Loyalist politicians.

A meeting on the Newtownards Road had been convened by the Combined Loyalist Command. The six UDA 'Brigadiers' sat down with their counterparts from the UVF to broker a deal.

Future military and criminal enterprises were discussed before a target for reprisal had been selected and a team made up of the best and most dedicated men from both the UVF and UDA.

The volunteers waited and occasionally glanced at the wall clock which showed it was approaching ten o'clock in the evening. The drawn curtains kept out the glow of the orange street lights.

The four men sat in an uneasy silence until, yet another stranger entered, his rabbit fur-lined blue parka drenched from the continuing storm. He dropped a heavy canvas bag on the floor before removing his sodden coat.

He opened the bag and began to issue the volunteers with their equipment for the upcoming operation. The UVF man, from Tiger Bay and with greasy hair, was given an AK47 assault rifle with two magazines full of ammunition. The magazines had been expertly taped together to help speed up reloading.

The assault rifle was one of the few which escaped capture when the security forces swooped on a huge arms consignment supplied by friends in South Africa.

The UDA Volunteer, from West Belfast, was handed the keys to a maroon VW Passat. The young man sitting next to him, from the South East Antrim UDA, was given a MAC 10 submachine gun and two South African hand grenades.

The bald guy cracking his fingers was the last man: he was also given a hand grenade and a 9mm Browning pistol which had been stolen from the British army many years before.

The men were then issued with blue boiler suits, surgical gloves, and black balaclavas. Each volunteer used a role of tape to cover the clothing gaps on their wrists, ankles and neck to stop any chance of leaving DNA at the future crime scene.

After quickly changing and checking their weapons the men sat and listened to the soft-spoken Ulsterman as he described the target for the night.

"Gentleman, tonight you are going to assassinate the man who has been organising the recent attacks against our people. Thomas McDaid is the Intelligence Officer of a dissident republican group."

"Which one?" the guy from Tiger Bay asked.

The Ulsterman looked at him coldly. He didn't ask for questions, nor did he expect any, so he was pissed off not only by the audacity but the tone.

"Continuity IRA, Real IRA, Dissident IRA, 'I can't believe it's' the fucking IRA! Does it fucking matter? He's a Fenian cunt who has planned and carried out attacks on the Loyalist community. If you don't like the job, fuck off now." He stared intently at the questioner.

Tom McDaid was a veteran PIRA volunteer who had, along with his colleagues, accepted the terms of the 1998 Good Friday Agreement. He was back to labouring and was making good money as a navvy.

The only link to the past that Tom didn't break was with his old handlers in the British Army's source unit.

For years Tom had been informing on members of the Belfast Brigade and the move from ArmaLite rifle to ballot box.

Now Tom made a bit of money on the side by keeping an eye on the young hotheads who drank in the Rock Bar and boasted of their exploits. It wasn't like that in his day: they would have been interrogated by the head of the nutting squad, the infamous Victor Secrillo, and his team of inquisitors.

The Provos Civilian Administration Unit were judge and jury, delivering any punishment they wanted to keep discipline in the community.

They were devoted to the rules of the IRA's Green Book the training and induction manual issued by the Irish Republican Army to all new recruits.

The Nutting Squad acted like religious zealots when dealing out their retribution. Secrillo's team would quickly get a confession out of any accused, even if the person being interrogated was innocent.

McDaid was a very poor choice of target. Not only was he nothing to do with recent attacks, but because he was an informer for the Security Forces his handlers were bound to protect him and unbeknown to all in the room less one. There was also another informer in play.

"He lives on the corner of Rodney Parade, so straight across the roundabout and then first left. It's directly opposite the Park Centre. This cheeky fucker has been working up in Carrickfergus on the housing project, so he has had plenty of time to recce plenty of targets in our homelands." The Ulsterman was building up in volume.

"His wife is one of the Connor family and his kids are probably involved as well, so waste every fucker in the house or anybody that comes to help," he ordered.

He then walked around the room and shook each volunteer's hand and took their mobile phones, promising to return them once they were back at the safe house.

The Park Centre was a modern-day mall built on the site of the old Celtic Park football and greyhound stadium. An army overt observation post sited on the roof of the Royal Victoria Hospital's nurses' home afford the security forces a panoramic view of the whole area.

The regular soldiers that usually manned the watchtower were tucked up safe in their beds for the night whilst members of a specialist surveillance unit took over observation of the area.

Two undercover soldiers carefully focused the large lens attached to a JVC video recorder whilst a third ensured that the lines of communication remained open between the Silver and Bronze tactical teams on the ground and the strategic Gold team decision makers back at headquarters.

The rain had stopped falling and the clouds had parted to reveal a bright full moon. Surveillance officers cleaned the windscreens of their vehicles to ensure they had optimum vision.

The rear of the centre was an ideal spot to hide and wait. A dark transit van with four soldiers in the back relaxed, listening to the radio commentary of the surveillance team following a maroon VW Passat.

A tall bald man dressed in all black played with the balaclava in his hand. He was getting the latest update of the movement of the approaching vehicle through a covert ear piece. He looked at the other members of Ulster Troop waiting in the back of the van and gave them a thumbs-up.

"Stand By, Stand By," he whispered, then pulled the balaclava over his face.

The Army handler of the Loyalist informer sat in the front of the van, hoping that his man remembered his instructions. If he didn't it was highly likely that the handler would be looking for another intelligence source.

"He'll shout 'Baboon' to identify himself. Just let him escape. He has a plausible cover story," the handler had told all the participants during the briefing.

A red BMW with two operators began driving down the hill from the Falls Road to intercept the hit team which was now manoeuvring around the roundabout on to the Donegall Road.

The men in the tower were giving a running commentary over the radio to ensure that everybody knew the precise location of the Passat. Back in the operation room senior police officers watched, occasionally making notes in their day books.

A black Audi with the surveillance team leader and the log keeper began to slowly ease forward from its hiding position by the service centre to eyeball the Passat as it left the roundabout and passed their location.

The final piece of the trap was a black, heavily armoured 4x4 Mercedes G Class with thick bumper bars. The two operators placed on crash helmets and neck braces and bit down onto their gum shields.

Ramming was a new tactic to the unit, but they had practised every possible scenario at a military complex on the coast at Ballykinler until they perfected their actions.

Senior officers from the PSNI had watched a demonstration and, along with members of their legal department, approved of the new response.

The orange street lights at the bottom of Rodney Parade had been shot out by pellets from an air rifle only minutes before the hit team started their journey.

The Passat began its left turn into Rodney Parade. A car with its lights on full beam was hurtling down the hill towards them, temporally blinding the driver and making him hesitate to make the turn when the Mercedes shot out of the darkened street and slammed into the front of the attacker's car with a horrible, bone jarring force.

The Passat was thrown into the middle of Donegall Road. The engine became deathly silent: the only noise was steam coming through the distorted radiator, and a smell of burnt rubber and leaking diesel.

The driver's legs, both broken in the impact, were trapped by the engine block which had been smashed off its mounting bolts and forced backwards towards the driving compartment.

The passenger seated directly behind the driver had a distorted bloody nose after face-butting the driver's head rest. He kicked at his door, which was crumpled and stuck fast because of the damage to the B piler between the driver's and passenger's doors.

The front seat passenger had dropped the MAC 10 submachine gun and one of the grenades which was rolling precariously along the distorted floor.

Above the sound of the driver's screams the other passengers could hear the screech of brakes, running footsteps, and English voices shouting.

"Get out of the car now, show me your hands!"

The man behind the driver scrambled for the AK47 and replaced the magazine, which had been dislodged during the crash. He then blindly fired a burst out of his window.

The staccato sounds of the 7.62mm rounds being fired in such a closed space further disorientated and deafened the volunteers.

The front seat passenger was young but an experienced UVF commander from Rathcoole. He quickly regained his composure. Realising he was being rapidly closed down he disengaged himself from both the airbag and his restraining seatbelt and staggered out of the door, grabbing the machine gun as he exited. He was quickly followed by the Volunteer from South East Antrim.

"Run, Davie, it's a trap!" the Antrim man screamed and ran away from the kid who was still in shock but trying to raise the tiny black MAC 10 in the direction of the onrushing soldiers.

"Army - halt or I fire!" shouted the arrest team.

Another long burst of bullets emanated from the back of the stricken vehicle. The guy with the AK was now leaning out of the window. He was groggy and shooting indiscriminately at the fleeting shadows.

A single shot was all it took to cure his concussion. A 5.56mm bullet fired from an HK 53 submachine gun hit Billy Kennedy from Tiger Bay square in the forehead. His brain and greasy hair were dispersed over the roof of the now smoking vehicle.

"Put the gun down, Davie," ordered the soldier with a Manchester accent who had jumped out of a black Audi.

The young commander appeared confused as on the other side of the Audi a girl was pointing a small black pistol towards him.

The man from Antrim ran towards a waiting black transit van. He had been told by his handler that they would provide salvation.

"Baboon, Baboon!" he shouted.

He was out of the killing zone so to add to his cover he fired the pistol he was carrying back towards the smoking car.

"Davie Smythe, we know all about you. You are surrounded. Put the gun down, you will not be harmed, I promise," the Manchester soldier shouted above the nose of the crackling as the car began to catch fire, its dead engine haemorrhaging from the ruptured fuel lines.

Two men wearing black crash helmets staggered from the Mercedes, which did not appear to have a scratch.

The Commander's situation was hopeless. He felt tears of defeat. What would his father think? A respected man in the Antrim farming community. He began to lower the machine gun when the crack of a bullet whizzed harmlessly past his left ear.

He staggered forward towards the soldiers.

"Don't shoot!" he screamed.

He turned to face the crack when a second bullet hit him in the throat, ripping out his trachea. The shock wave formed by the heavy 9mm bullet destroyed the anterior jugular vein and carotid artery. A large flap of bloody skin hung down like a child's bib.

Sticky red liquid was propelled into the sky as the young man's heart pumped rapidly. He first dropped to his knees, then slumped face-first on to the tarmac.

The bald Antrim volunteer was panting when he reached the van. His handler grabbed him by the shoulders and slammed him into the side of the black vehicle with a deafening bang.

He ripped off his agent's black balaclava.

"What the fuck are you doing? I expressly told you no shooting. You have DNA on the pistol and gunshot residue on your body. Fuck off back to your masters and I'll do what I can to sort this shit out. Get rid of the gun and lay low until I contact you."

The man was grinning as he started to jog towards the roundabout and the safety of the Village. He then felt a red-hot sting in his thigh and fell hard on to the cold wet pavement.

The tall soldier approached him and yanked him to his feet.

"What the fuck? I work for you. I shouted 'Baboon', you deaf bastard."

Sergeant Dave Wildman removed his balaclava, then grabbed the bleeding man by the throat. His eyes were burning with rage. The orange streetlights shone off both their bald heads.

"You're a fucking grass, lowest of the low and now you have just killed one of your own. I shot you as a bit of insurance. The Brigadiers are going to be looking for a grass - at least if you go back injured you might survive their questioning. It's a flesh wound, so stop crying."

The big Wiganer slapped him around the face, then pointed in the direction of the Village.

"Go!"

Screams were coming from the car as the ambush team wrestled with the driver's door, then faced the problem of trying to get his crushed leg from the clamp of the engine block.

In the distance a fire engine's siren was heard. The heat from the car was becoming intense and the rescuers were forced to back off.

The passenger from the BMW arrived with a green army fire extinguisher which was followed by the one from the Audi.

The driver's screams turned into whimpers and then fell silent as he drifted into unconsciousness. The small gathering crowd looked on helplessly as the firemen cut the driver's body from the wreckage.

"Going to be a busy night doing paperwork, Johnno," the tall Wiganer shouted across to the Mancunian team leader.

"Fuck off, Dave! Go and have another gingerbread man, you wanker," was Johnno's reply.

The SAS Sergeant, although a fitness fanatic, was a sucker for the ginger treats.

The Loyalist operation was a complete disaster. Not only had they lost three good volunteers, but they had also shown a complete inability to conduct a worthwhile attack in a Republican area. The command structure was archaic, and the units riddled with informers.

The volunteer that escaped was completely exonerated after being debriefed by a commander from the UDA and one from the UVF. His wound was compelling, but not as much as the cash both debriefers were being paid by their security forces handlers.

McDaid and his family were safe and were never under any threat, as he had been moved to a new home on the Poleglass estate in South Belfast the week before.

The security forces had decided to step in to protect the innocent family that now lived at the corner house on Rodney Parade.

The other part of the plan was to give the commander of the South East Antrim unit more credence within the ranks of the UDA. Time would only tell if that part of the strategy came to fruition.

CHAPTER ONE

Jumbles Country Park, Bolton, 2018

The morning ground mist had begun to be melted away by the new day's warmth of a freshly rising sun. It was a spectacular sunrise: the rays of light reflected off the clear water of the reservoir through the trees which were covered in new colourful blossom. Spring had brought growth and life after a cold depressing winter.

A slight breeze gently caressed the thinner branches, making them slowly dance in rhythm, and made the water ripple.

Chaz White called out to the bundle of brown fur crashing through the bushes. Her brown coat was shining wet - she had probably been in the water chasing ducks again. He was convinced that she was part spaniel, part woolly aquatic creature.

He faintly heard the scrunch of footsteps heading in his direction along the sandstone track from the direction of the tree-lined artificial lake.

Cautiously he scanned his surroundings. Above him the sky was a clear blue, only marked by vapour trails from high-flying jets, whisking holidaymakers to distant lands.

Soon it would be time for his annual trip to Turkey, he thought, then reminded himself to book the kennels for the dog.

The figure walking towards him was tall and wearing dark clothing. They had appeared in the distance, head down walking with purpose, hands thrust into the front pouch of a black hooded top.

He couldn't see if the stranger was walking a dog or carrying a lead. Chaz was always fearful for his boisterous three-year-old springer. She had been attacked before in the park and he didn't need any further vets' bills.

"Tilly, biscuit!" he called to try and get the dog to return to his side.

A chestnut brown head appeared from the long grass and raced towards the invitation, pink tongue swinging out of its ever-hungry mouth.

Chaz knelt and placed the choker chain around the happy mutt's neck. He lovingly stroked her as he heard the footsteps of the approaching man. Tilly lovingly looked up into her master's eyes, waiting on his next command or offer of a tasty treat.

Happy that the dog was secure he stood up and faced the stranger, a man. He was head and shoulders taller than Chaz, slim, pale with long bony hands. A black hood concealed his face which was set back into the shadow made by the material.

"Where is Johnno, Whitey?" His voice was familiar, reedy, and nervous.

"Who the fuck are you?" Chaz asked, then began to realise that he did recognise the man in front of him.

"Sorry, Whitey," the man said.

"Sorry for what?"

The tall man drew his right arm back, then slashed at Chaz's throat with a matt black karambit knife. The razor-sharp curved blade easily sank into the soft flesh below the victim's left ear and made a half-moon path, tracing the line below Chaz's jaw.

The karambit, an agricultural knife, was designed to be used by farmers raking in roots and threshing rice plants. It resembled a tiger's claw and was just as devastating.

The cold sting in Chaz's throat began to warm up and bright red blood started to ooze through the wound. He tried to clasp the cut to stem the sticky blood which began to forcefully pump through his fingers.

"Why?" he gasped.

He fell to his knees, the sound of his dog whimpering in his ears. A savage blow from the finger ring at the butt of the knife into his face whiplashed his skull backwards, further opening the jugular and carotid arteries.

The attacker was now in darkness. Chaz's heart was in overdrive as his adrenalin rushed, sending his brain into a fight or flight mode. Two actions which he would now never take. His arm was pulling as Tilly tried in vain to drag her master away.

There was a yelp and the pulling on his wrist stopped. He slumped forward into the pool of his own blood.

Longsight, Manchester.

Phil 'Buster' Johnston turned the page of his book then looked out through the massing rain drops on the windscreen. The morning had been quite pleasant for Manchester, with the sun poking through the grey clouds. Now the deluge had begun like monsoon time in Java. 'If it's not raining it's not training,' he thought.

He was hoping that the technical unit that was trying to find a position to install a covert camera to cover the front door of the address would work a bit quicker.

Sitting out on a suburban street in Manchester watching a drug dealer's front door was not a healthy option with the number of spotters that roamed or rode the estates.

"No Change, No Change," he gave over the covert radio cunningly concealed in his grimy surveillance van.

He could envisage the rest of his team turning down the volume on their media devices or reaching to grab a bookmark in case Buster 'The Eyeball' had seen movement from the address.

"No Change, Buster," came the reply from Little B in the operations room back in central Manchester. Her voice was bright and cheerful, as was her manner.

He reached down for his book again.

"Buster, are you in a position to take a call?" Little P shouted up.

"Yes, yes, anytime for you," he replied as he placed his page marker back into his book. Just three more chapters until he could throw his latest Jack Reacher novel into the team cupboard.

He was about twenty Reacher books in and was getting to know the fictional character better than the members of his own team.

He always flirted with Little B - in fact all the male members of the team, and some of the female ones also, toyed with her, knowing that her boyfriend, Ched, would be sitting beside her observing remote CCTV feeds or monitoring any incidents taking place in the vicinity of the day's operation.

Today Ched was reduced to watching the back gate of the address.

His mobile blurted out a chirping song.

He looked at his watch, an old CWS G1098 which he managed to keep hold of when he left the army. It was coming up to two o'clock in the afternoon. The animals would soon be waking and making their way into town to feed.

The prey at this time of year was students new to the city. Fresh faced and unwary of the hard-arsed feral estate kids who would rob them of their cash, phones, and designer trainers.

If the South Manchester kids didn't rob them, they would sell the freshers any drug they wished to consume, from acetylfentanyl to yaba. The latest drug of choice was fentanyl, a synthetic opioid which was about to become an epidemic amongst the academics.

The dealers loaded up their produce supplied from the local wholesaler. Sometimes they cut and mixed the drugs even further to feed their own habit or increase the profit.

Most of the users were getting less than forty percent of what they were purchasing, which on reflection was probably a godsend as better purity would probably kill them, or at least lead to irrevocable brain damage.

They were content in their ignorance that the substance they were sniffing or pumping in their veins was mixed with, laxatives, rat poison or talcum powder.

Students brought a lot of revenue to the city and a recent spate of overdoses had started to reflect badly on the Mayor and the Police Force as the local rag's initial reporting had started to make the middle pages of the national red tops and were quickly moving forward towards the front page.

The local wholesaler, Damien 'Damo' Franks, was the top jockey of the LSL, 'The Longsight Legion.' He was twenty-three and living the dream.

A shiny brand-new Mercedes GLC SUV sat outside his doorway after being recently re-skinned to a redwood colour and the windows tinted.

When he appeared, he dressed in designer clothes and always wore the ubiquitous bling of heavy gold neck chains, bracelets, and watches.

A shaved head, dark glasses, tattooed body, and hours spent in the gym made him appear as a hard man but, as in most of the criminals Buster had followed, they were just jumped-up punks, bullies that had never been slapped down or challenged.

His street soldiers had no father figures or role models in their lives. Mothers that were too busy trying to put food on the table for her army of siblings or out late turning tricks or trying to get another hit to make her mundane life pass with greater ease.

Damo recruited kids from the local schools to stand on street corners and watch for "Da Feds". They ran drugs and guns through the estates to the next link in the chain, the street dealers who were in turn controlled by the enforcers who were pushing to move up a rung to be a Lieutenant, a member of Damo's inner circle.

Buster hit a button on the dashboard to operate his mobile.

"You're fucking gorgeous, B. How's that wanker Ched?"

She giggled down the line: "Sat beside me. No change on that front."

Her accent betrayed her Wigan roots. B had been on the team and trained by Buster when she first applied to become a surveillance officer.

"I bet you wish it was me sat beside you," he teased.

Little B was a good operator and had been moved back into the operations room after her promotion to Sergeant.

"When are you going to retire so I can get back out on the ground?" she goaded.

He smiled. "No time soon, darlin'. You know I love getting more overtime than the Chief Constable and love fucking up these crims' lives."

A car rolled to a stop in front of the Mercedes.

"Stand By, Stand By, black BMW 5 series is a stop, stop, stop, outside the subject address. VRM is Lima India Papa Sierra 69. Unknown female from the driver's seat towards the address. Long blonde shoulder length hair." He stopped midway through the commentary.

The concealed camera in the van quickly focused and took a dozen pictures of the visitor.

He was laughing as he began the commentary again.

"She's wearing a long expensive-looking fur coat which has just blown open and I can confirm that there is no fur on show beneath it."

The radio jumped to life with requests to swap position and calling him a lucky or a lying bastard.

"Sorry, B, where were we," he asked, still chuckling.

"I was just ringing up to tell you that he was going to get a visit from an escort. He's cancelled his trip to see the Cranwell's in Liverpool, so that's job done for the day. LIPS 69 will be seeing to his every need for a grand an hour."

"Thanks, B, see you back at the debrief. Get a brew on and I'll bring the cakes."

He pressed the phone button and immediately switched to the radio.

"That's a wrap for the day, chaps and chapesses. Back to HQ for a debrief acknowledge in order."

He slowly manoeuvred the van along the terraced street and took a last look at the two expensive cars outside the armoured front door covered by security lights and cameras.

The big hardman was too scared to leave his manor. He was safe in his own little fiefdom, acting like a feudal lord. Happy and safe in his own little stream but not brave enough to venture into the open sea where the big sharks lurked.

He turned the local radio on to catch the latest news. He could visualise the other members of his team putting away laptops after watching Netflix or the latest box sets. Or Janey closing the surveillance log and putting away her knitting.

They would soon be racing to beat the rush hour traffic and get the debrief done before submitting their day's expenses paperwork.

The radio reporter was a local woman. Buster had met her in a local bar: raven hair and sad smile from too many bad dates.

"Breaking news from Bolton. A man's body has been discovered in a local beauty spot."

Buster turned to find some music; he'd had enough crime for one day.

Jumbles Country Park, Bolton

Janet Wood peered inside the white tent. The man and his dog were entwined in death.

After dressing in her white disposable suit and putting on blue plastic gloves she had been briefed by one of her Detectives and signed in to the taped off site, carefully stepping on the laid-out blocks towards the incident.

Beside the bodies a crime scene investigator meticulously took photographs, then placed items into evidence bags, only stopping the process to give each bag an evidence number and reference to the photo frame.

The camera flashed and the aperture shutter clicked as it captured the scene.

The CSI looked up, only his eyes visible and teary. He was embalmed in a white over-suit with blue plastic bags over his boots and latex gloves. His face was covered by a mask and his head by the suit's hood.

Outside a generator was humming as it powered the lighting system.

"How are you doing, Griz?" she asked.

She had worked with Steve 'Griz' Adams for many years. It seemed to her that he was the SOCO at every crime scene she had ever attended. He could be grouchy if you stepped off his designated approach line or asked any stupid questions.

He stared at her for a moment: flecks of blonde hair were visible escaping from her hood.

"Look, Boss, I get it; you know, people murdering people. Some deserve it, or they are done in as a consequence of their wealth or an item they are carrying, but why kill the fucking dog?"

She nodded in agreement. "I take it you haven't lifted them yet then."

"Just about to," he sighed.

He placed the SLR camera down on an area he had previously cleared and knelt to the side of the body, slowly pulling the now stiff corpse by its right shoulder till it lifted on to its left side. There were small peeling sounds as the man's face broke away from the congealed blood.

DCI Wood was the syndicate head of team two FMIT. The Force Major Incident Team were always on 24/7 notice to deploy to murders, kidnappings, serious assaults, and every other incident which the senior leadership team bracketed as a 'Major Incident.'

FMIT was a large unit packed with Detectives, analysts, researchers and subject specialists in firearms and communications. There were eight syndicates to cover Greater Manchester, but it was still not nearly enough. Some jobs were put on the back burner as other crimes hit the already over-worked teams and often top trumped long running investigations.

Janet had been with her team for eight months and the case load was already overwhelming. The Senior Investigating Officer had been putting pressure on all his syndicate leaders to get results and get the workload down. Everybody knew that the boss was getting shit from the Chief and shit only travelled one way, downwards.

The bright mobile halogen lights were warm on DCI Wood's back as she examined the wound, a slice along the victim's neck resembling a macabre smile. Dried blood along the sides of the cut made the injury even more gruesome, like thick lipstick administered by a mad makeup artist.

The victim's skin was grey, his eyes partially open and black. Pieces of grit were engrained into his forehead.

She took his hands and carefully examined them. They were cold, like a waxwork mannikin's.

"No self-defence wounds, so he had no warning about the attack," she mentioned.

Griz carefully placed the body on its back.

"What's that lapel badge he's wearing?" he pointed out.

Stuck on the right breast of the man's burgundy fleece jacket was a small bronze badge. A circle with flames coming out topped with a red and white plume.

"It looks like something military, perhaps he's an ex-soldier. Get a picture of it and I'll disseminate it to Inspector Jones who runs the Armed Forces Champions in GMP."

She touched the fur of the dog. Like her owner she was cold.

DCI Wood left the tent and removed her mask, the smell of dried blood and death still in her nostrils.

CHAPTER TWO

The City Cemetery, West Belfast

The lawns were immaculately manicured and well laid out. The Victorian graveyard had been the final resting place for the people of Belfast since 1865.

The one hundred and one acres of land stretched from the Falls Road, following the line of the Whiterock Road as it rose towards Turf Lodge. Over to the south lay Falls Park, a popular area for dog walkers, joggers and local families exercising their children.

Two men in dark clothing entered the graveyard from Whiterock Road. The older man was in his seventies, stooped, walking slowly. His younger companion had darting eyes, looking for threats behind every gravestone.

The old man flipped his head.

"You probably only know Pat O'Hare's playground as a place your Ma pushed you on the swing, Phelan. Back in the day that was Pegasus Park or McCrory Park a base for the Brits."

The younger man had other matters on his hands trying to guard the head of Republican intelligence.

They slowly walked down the hill towards the Glen Lodge cemetery office. To their right was the resting places for almost two hundred and twenty-five thousand people of all denominations.

There was a Protestant patch, a Jewish plot 'Bathaiym,' and scores of other religions mixed with the majority Catholics.

The gate they had entered was known locally as the Poor Gate. Eighty thousand unmarked pauper graves were also in the grounds. The 'Poor Grounds' were in a less scenic part of the cemetery. No headstones, and families were not buried together, unlike their rich masters six feet down in the 'Property Graves' which, back in the day, cost anything from one to nine pounds and were adorned with sandstone Gothic vaults or elaborate head stones.

Even in death, rich and poor went their separate ways. The rich had their urns, obelisks, and angles, the paupers just the grass and trees above their bones.

Now rabbits played and birds sang overhead. It was a picture of tranquillity.

"We used to hide our guns and bombs with the rich bastards," the old man chuckled.

They passed a white war grave, a soldier that was resting in peace after making the ultimate sacrifice during the Somme.

"Uncle Sammy," the old man pointed out.

"You had an uncle that fought for the Brits?"

The old man looked at the lad with contempt.

"Know your history, boy! There are scores of brave souls in here that fought against tyranny. Why shouldn't they lay at peace with their own kind?"

Two other men entered the main entrance on the junction of the Falls and Whiterock Road. One wore dark glasses - he believed it made him look menacing. In truth he was quaking.

He was also a bodyguard, but in way above his head. Pumping iron and taking steroids did not make him a hard man. He was now in the middle of West Belfast. Enemy territory.

His companion had a bald head and walked with a limp: he had dark eyes, no feeling, no soul.

The bodyguard walking down the hill spotted them first. He looked for any creases or bulges in the clothing of the bodybuilder.

He had no fear of the opposition and was happy in the knowledge that a back-up car was waiting on the junction of St James Road with four other armed men in case the meeting didn't go as planned.

The stone tower by the entrance was the only remains of the old mortuary chapel. Benches were arranged in the open area. Some had brass plaques, donated by relatives that had found tranquillity in visiting their loved ones.

The bald man offered his hand, It was not accepted. The old man pointed to a bench; they sat side by side. The guards stood at either end mainly sizing each other up. Two alpha males separated by two old lions.

The old man looked out from his seat, not looking at his visitor.

"Bobby, you have some balls to come here so you must be desperate. What can I do for you?"

The Loyalist cleared his throat, "Thanks for meeting me, Sean. Makes a change from shouting threats at each other through the bars at the Maze. How times change. Do you miss those times?"

The Republican stared into the distance. The traffic was building up on the Falls, black taxis dispensed their passengers and ferried away for their next pick up.

"Do I miss being at war, waiting for my home to be invaded, stopped, and searched on the street, looking under my car to see if you or your friends had put a bomb under it? No, I don't miss it."

"But do you think the people really appreciate what we have done for our communities? We were big men, guardians of our communities, now what are we? Old has-beens ridiculed by the youth, some say overtaken, rusty guns!"

"Spit it out, Bobby," the old man demanded.

The Loyalist nervously cracked his fingers.

"Let's just ramp the tension up again, over the summer say. Get the Peelers working overtime. Stuff in the papers just to show that we haven't gone away, and we are still looking after our people."

The old man looked at the Loyalist with disdain.

"You want to go back to violence just to gain some long-lost credibility? My organisation is very happy with the equilibrium at the moment, the ballot box has been very beneficial. Perhaps you should tell your masters that."

"No, not violence as such, just sabre rattling, say a few demos up on the peace line. Bit of disorder during the parades, jazz it up a bit, you know - 'heightened tension' as that new chief Peeler keeps saying when he comes on the news."

"All the while poor Nationalist youths will be arrested and homes in the Ardoyne will have their windows smashed."

"Think about it, Sean. We could then come together as peace makers. One last hoorah. Two senior statesmen bringing our communities back together. What do you say?"

"I say you sound like a politician. I've thought about it, and you do not and will not have the support of the Republican movement. Also, I'll warn you now that if you try and induce us in to any retaliatory actions, we will only target one person. Goodbye, Bobby. Good luck with your political agenda."

The old man stood up and walked back up the hill. His bodyguard remained in position, watching the Loyalist leave the gate. A red saloon appeared and whisked them away north towards the safety of the Shankill.

"What was all that about?" he asked when he re-joined the old man.

"Just a draught, son, a cold wind from the past that might need to be excluded before everybody catches a cold."

The Stephen Oakes Briefing Room, Manchester

The debrief had started well until Buster downloaded the pictures of the leggy blonde escort and placed them in front of the team. The log keeper Janey was trying to talk through all the events of the day's surveillance but was being drowned out by wolf whistles and banter.

Buster slammed his fist on to the large circular table.

"Hey, calm down, get your heads on, and listen in. Let's get the log done, then we can discuss tomorrow's job. We're back on that armed robbery team in Salford, so switch on."

The room immediately fell silent. Ten police surveillance officers sat like admonished schoolchildren, red-faced and scared to look around at their peers.

He was one of them, but then again, he was not. His pathway to the team had been much longer and far more diverse. They were police officers with warrants and powers of arrest. He was police staff with an authorisation from the Chief Constable that he could break traffic laws when following a suspect.

The most senior members of the team had been with him for around seven years whereas he had now entered his fifteenth year on the Surveillance unit.

His life had begun on Langworthy Road in Salford before moving to the high-rise flats of George Brown House. As a Salford street urchin, he ran with the younger siblings of the notorious Burrows and Potter families.

After his father died on the docks and his mother turned to drink, he moved out of the 'city within a city' to live with his granddad in a mining town called Tyldesley.

Old Pops Johnston was an old soldier, but he would do his morning walk followed by one hundred push ups and one hundred sit ups.

"Been for your morning run and swim in the canal, Pops?" the young Phillip Johnston would ask.

"Only five miles today, lad," the old man would reply before walking Phil to the school gates.

Phil loved walking to school with his granddad who was a war veteran. They spoke incessantly about the army and his visits to far-flung countries.

People stepped aside and some people appeared to hold the old man in high esteem. Women young and old would often stop Johnston senior and ask what he was up to or if he was going to attend a local event.

"You never lose it, son. That's why your Grandma passed away - I wore her out," he joked.

It seemed only natural that Phil would follow his grandfather's footsteps and enlist in the Lancashire Fusiliers. When he marched into the recruiting office in Bolton, he was surprised to find out that the Lancashire's had been amalgamated with three other Fusilier Regiments to become the Royal Regiment of Fusiliers.

It was the proudest day of his life when he marched off the drill square in front of his beaming Pops, who was wearing his beret with a bright primrose yellow hackle. A rack of medals shone brightly on his chest.

He may have been old, but he was still fit, strong and proud. He would not have looked out of place marching alongside the young soldiers on parade.

At the reception afterwards Granddad was the centre of attention as usual. He was surrounded by members of the training staff who stood in line to shake his hand.

"Johnston, get your sorry arse over here, lad."

It was the dulcet tones of Company Sergeant Major Noble who was also a Fusilier.

"You never mentioned that your grandfather was a regimental legend." The CSM appeared to be admonishing the young soldier.

Johnston said nothing.

Sergeant Ron Owen was the next one to have a dig.

"Do you recognise the medals he's wearing?"

Phil stuttered, "I've seen them and polished them a thousand times, Sarge, but I never asked what they were for."

The Sergeant's eyes appeared to enlarge.

"There is saus SARGE, Mas SARGE, and back Pas SARGE, but no Sarge in the army, you little scrote."

Phil's granddad and the CSM were roaring with laughter.

Nobby Noble put a hand on the lad's shoulder and then pointed to each shining bauble on his granddad's chest.

"That is a Queens Gallantry Medal, the one next to it is the Military Medal. Notice it has a bronze oak leaf, which is another story altogether."

He then pointed to the medal at the start of the line. The ribbon was dark crimson with a navy-blue band down the centre broken only by a silver bar in the middle.

His finger hovered above it as if he were scared to touch it.

"And that one I have heard in folklore around the campfire was presented by a member of the Royal Family in a closed audience with the citation read only once before being placed back into a safe."

Granddad nodded in acknowledgement but appeared uneasy with the story.

Phil joined his Battalion and quickly found his niche working with the reconnaissance platoon. Working in small teams in front of the larger rifle companies his patrol lived on their wits to close with the enemy and find out their dispositions and weaknesses before reporting back to their commanders' planning attacks.

A deployment to Northern Ireland enhanced his covert training by joining the Close Observation Platoon, learning new clandestine techniques then testing them to the full, hiding close to terrorists as they prepared to attack security force patrols.

He learned how to take covert photographs and videos, then prepare them for court proceedings.

He loved the two years in Ireland, the adrenalin rushes, the highs of a successful job and the famous piss-ups after an operation concluded.

He had just been promoted to Corporal when he noticed a sign on Battalion Orders asking for volunteers for 'Special Duties' back in Northern Ireland.

He had at times worked with a shadowy unit who called themselves the SSU. Unlike the COP the Special Surveillance Unit hardly ever wore uniform. Their hair was long, and they drove out of camp in civilian vehicles.

The notice intrigued him, so he phoned his mentor: his granddad.

Granddad knew all about the SSU and its founding fathers back in the early '70s because he had been one of its earliest volunteers.

Buster's move to the special duties would eventually cost him his marriage and any close contact with his two kids. Phil had also found that he was more like his granddad than he had ever thought. He attracted women and he could never say 'no'.

Long undercover tours of duty in Northern Ireland were broken by short training periods and moves up the promotion ladder. After being promoted to Sergeant Phil was posted back to his Battalion with orders to rest up. Someone at manning and records had overlooked that Phil's unit was due to return to Ulster.

During a chance vehicle stop on a lonely road outside Cullyhanna in South Armagh he bumped into a former SSU colleague working on a covert operation. The word soon got back to the Unit's commander that Johnno was in the Province.

A week later he was still in Ireland but not in uniform. He was with his old surveillance team based in Fermanagh whilst his wife packed up their married quarters in Ballykinler and prepared to be moved back to the mainland.

The unit was now being referred to as 'The Det' and the members of the team were 'Operators' They specialised in covert surveillance by foot or vehicle. They were experts in the use of technical devices and remaining invisible to their surroundings.

The Det had quickly developed into an elite surveillance unit. They had begun to branch out and become involved in support operations with the Special Air Service and the Security Service.

The skill set of the unit's operators was much in demand. Johnno was later offered a two-year secondment to the Metropolitan Police, then the plum posting to the School of Police Covert Tactics in Bedfordshire.

Phil's army career was rushing to a close. His pension as a Warrant Officer was good but would not pay his every bill. He was now divorced after too many nights away and too many women sharing his bed.

As luck would have it one of his former pupils at the school in Bedfordshire had recently taken over as the Detective Chief Inspector of the Greater Manchester Surveillance Unit and asked him to attend an interview.

The DCI was a drinking mate of a Superintendent who happened to be close to an Acting Chief Constable, who had the ear of the Chief Constable.

The ACC found a loophole which would allow a civilian to become an active member of the police force.

Section 38 Police Reform Act specified that a Chief Constable could grant certain designated powers of a constable, mainly to civilian detectives but special dispensation could be given to people with a 'Specialist skill set' to help Operational effectiveness.

His vetting was at the highest level possible, he was an instructor for foot and vehicle surveillance. Covert rural surveillance was his speciality and he had years of experience in planning and conducting high risk operations.

He was now fifty-five, his nearest colleague in age around the table was thirty-eight and classed as an old timer. Buster, as he was now known, ran his Bronze team hard. Some complained that their colleagues in the Yellow team had an easy ride.

On training days, they trained for the full shift, unlike the Yellows that completed their vehicle checks and paperwork before going to the nearest bar.

Buster told any dissenters that he would happily let them leave or let them move to the Yellows. He reminded them that all the Senior Officers asked for the Bronze team when the most important jobs went down.

That was the reason they got the most overtime, the best cars and equipment and the best intelligence feeds to lock up the bad guys.

The meeting came to an end and Buster reminded them about the following day's activities before approaching Fleur, the youngest member of the team. She had shown great initiative on the arduous pre-select course and with Buster's tuition had easily passed her advanced driving and surveillance courses.

"How's it going?" he asked.

"Good, living the dream," she smiled.

"Fancy a drink or a bite to eat?"

"Not tonight, Buster, he's not on nights. Maybe later in the week."

"No problem, it's just I can't make my mind up between a halloumi salad or chippy tea. I thought you might be able to help me decide."

"I suppose I could take a quickie detour via your house," she giggled.

Hilton Park Service Station, M6

The three young boys who appeared scared, and lonely, hadn't spoken to each all journey. They sat on separate seats and only looked out of the darkened windows of the minibus. The two men in the front had promised them they were going on an adventure when they woke them early from the locked bedroom.

They had been given a uniform from a school which none of them had ever attended. They were not related or even from the same town. The oldest was eight, tall for his age and skinny. He had been living in a home in Drogheda after his grandmother, his only living relative, died.

The middle one was chubby, with red cheeks from running around his father's farm before the old man suffered a fatal heart attack and the small one had freckles, a Belfast boy: junkie mother, father unknown.

The driver and his mate had been kind. They got them onto the ship without anybody knowing through secret gates, then off without any checks. They had given them pop, crisps, and sweets while they sat in the darkness in the bowels of the huge ship.

Now they had brought back a feast from Burger King, and they all tucked in as the vehicle pulled away from the service station.

They were going to a new home on the mainland, they had said. Rich men would buy them to join their families, educate them and give them presents.

"I need to pee!"

The co-driver turned, "Ya pee in the plastic bottle, Freckles, we told you that. Keep smiling, pretty boy. These old fellas are going to pay a good price for you."

The Half Moon Pub, Tyldesley

It was late in the evening when Phil walked into the Half Moon. A few of the regulars were glued to a screen watching a football match, oohing and aahing as overpaid prima donnas kicked a ball about.

At the far end of the bar stood his granddad, pint of Guinness in hand and in deep conversation with Ali, the barmaid. He could not hear the conversation, but it was obviously gripping the voluptuous woman.

"Hey, old fella, stop chatting that young lady up. At your age it could be fatal."

The old man turned to greet his prodigy. "Yes, son, but if she dies, she dies."

It was an old line which they had used for many years, but still got a chuckle.

"And who are you calling a lady, Phil? I bet your granddad could still curl my toes," Ali said.

"I'm sure he'd have a good try, but these days it takes four blokes to lift him on top of a woman and six to lift him off."

Ali looked puzzled. "Why do they need two more lads to lift him off?" she asked.

"Ah, he puts up a fight," Phil retorted, trying to stop his eyes wandering down to her thrusting cleavage.

"Fuck off, Phil, he's still got a twinkle in his eye."

"And an industrial supply of blue pills, so be careful, babe."

Granddad was beaming. The twinkle, though a little faded, was still in his eye.

Phil grabbed his pint and showed his Granddad to an empty stall.

"Have you been to church today, son?" It was quite a left field question. The last time that either of them had been to a church was his Mum's funeral which was over ten years ago.

"Are you losing your marbles, Pops? I finished work and went for a run, then the gym, and now I'm talking to you."

"No, son, no, it's just I nipped to your flat before and I heard someone praying to God and shouting for Jesus."

"What are you doing skulking around my property, Pops?"

The old man smiled.

"Old habits die hard, son. I saw an unusual car outside your door, and I decided to have a nosey. Just like the old days back in Belfast." He took a gulp of the black liquid.

"Well, you can't get away with it these days, you have to fill in paperwork. Bosses need to sign authorities before you even set foot on the ground, and that's both over here and in the Province. You can't just mount an operation on a whim, even if it's just to watch your grandson shagging lovely Colleen. I should lock you up for being a pervert."

"I'm no perv, but I do agree she was lovely. I saw her from the park when she was leaving. Off to get her husband's tea on, I suppose. You should go back to Sharon and the kids. Get your family back again. It's not too late to start again."

"Pops, she's moved on. I've moved on. She's married to a nice bloke. Yes, he was a Royal Signals officer, but I can overlook that as he's been a good stepdad. The kids are grown up and well balanced, so I have no issues at all with life."

"Except still thinking you're twenty-one and tickling anything with a skirt. Including Scotsmen."

"For fuck's sake, Pops - pot, kettle, black. I am your younger reflection."

They both leaned back and laughed.

The football had finished, and the punters returned to the bar to discuss formations and tactics they would have used if they had been the multi-millionaire manager of the team instead of a gas fitter or a plasterer.

Ali switched over the channel to the local news. A bulletin showed a windswept reporter doing a piece about a local man from Bolton and his dog who had been brutally murdered that morning.

Phil had just returned from the bar before Ali called last orders.

"Do you think the war will ever start again, son?"

"Which war? The Gulf, World War!"

"Over the water, back in Ireland. It was a bad time on all sides. '73 was horrendous - we had to fight fire with fire. No authorities or even rules in them days, son."

"It wasn't a war to people over here, Pops. An 'Internal Security Operation' they called it. Even the people over there call it the Troubles and not a war. I think it's over and I for one hope it is. Too many people lost or are still suffering. There are individuals that would want it to go back to the ArmaLite but thankfully the ballot box has won. Who says the politicians know fuck all? It looks like they got that one right."

When his granddad found out that Phil had passed selection and joined the Det he was over the moon.

The Det had been born from the bastard loins of the Military Reaction Force, an off the record group of soldiers conducting clandestine operations with little oversight.

The new descendants in the lineage had come under a structured training regime after a vigorous selection process conducted by members of the SAS and Intelligence specialists.

The unit had grown from a twenty-man squad based behind a wriggly tin barricade in the middle of Palace Barracks to one hundred and fifty men and women split into three geographical detachments covering the Brigade areas. These Detachments became known as North, South and East Det.

The MRF had followed the teachings of General Sir Frank Kitson, an expert in low intensity warfare. The General was Belfast Brigade Commander in the early '70s and had been quick to adapt tactics that had previously been used in Kenya and Cyprus. Counterinsurgency, Psyops, Pseudo gangs and Informants were the buzz words.

Sir Frank had also championed the use of Special Forces and Paramilitary counter gangs.

Hearts and minds were the hymn he preached but the carrot or the stick was the practice carried out by his newly formed unit, the MRF, who were tasked to gather intelligence and find insurgents that were willing to talk.

A darker side to the organisation were the Q Squad who drove into Nationalist enclaves to shoot known terrorists or to stir up trouble in the community.

Phil's grandfather had seen action before going to Northern Ireland, but only Ireland gave him recurring panic attacks.

Nexus House, Ashton Under Lyne

Sharon Croft looked at her almost blank i2 association chart. The only icons she had placed on the A3 sheet were a body with the name Charles White, his date of birth and 'VICTIM' plus the location.

The icon was a body, no soul, no history of its past life and loves.

The end of the pen top she was chewing was getting a little stale. It was a habit she subconsciously performed when in deep concentration.

She looked at another screen and looked at the growing list of actions being allocated to the Syndicate's detectives by the office manager. Her list of actions to be completed for the office manager was at that moment quite small, so she opened the file listing the exhibits and noticed something of interest.

DCI Wood looked over her spectacles into the open plan office and watched the progress of her senior analyst as she weaved between the desks towards her office.

She could guarantee that within the next five minutes she would be giggling no matter how grave the matter was.

"Morning, Boss, I've just noticed an item listed on the exhibits list as a military badge, but no further description."

Janet was impressed, that was possibly one of the longest sentences she had heard Sharon say without a swear word.

"I didn't know you were ex-military, Sharon?"

"I wasn't, but that twat of an ex-husband was. I know a few badges after being an army wife so I thought I would have a look."

The DCI rummaged through a pile of manilla folders and photobooks on her creaking desk.

She eventually found the exhibit folder and leafed through the file until she found the picture of the small bronze badge with a circle with flames coming out topped with a red and white plume.

"Royal Regiment of Fusiliers, Boss," Sharon proudly shouted.

"That was my ex's old unit." She added.

Janet thought about the information. "Is your ex still in the Army? He might know the victim."

"No, he's been out of the army a while and away from that Regiment for even longer. He works for the DSU now. Phil Johnston."

"Buster Johnston, the team leader from the Dedicated Surveillance Unit?" Janet thought back to a briefing she had received from the very charismatic man.

"The very same twat. We divorced and I remarried to become a Croft, but he remained a twat."

Her boss giggled.

"Just going off the subject, Sharon, why is he called Buster?"

Sharon smiled as she recounted the story.

"Everyone on the DSU has a handle they use on the radio. It is easier to remember and quicker than shouting out a call sign when the log keeper is trying to make notes. When they join the unit, they have a scrum down and they choose a name for the new guy. It's very politically incorrect, but nobody gives a fuck. One bald guy was called Chemo, Timex got his name because he was always late on plot, McGowan has no fucking teeth and Buster was because he looked like somebody's bulldog."

That was the version which Phil 'Buster' Johnston had given her.

The real reason Buster was the chosen handle for Phil was because one of the females on the team had said that when she was on her surveillance course her instructor, Phil, was like a dog with a bone and, like her Staffordshire bull terrier Buster, he would shag a rolling doughnut.

Sharon leafed through more pictures in the scene of evidence book. She stopped and stared at a graphic shot of the dead man's face and the gruesome injury.

She turned the page to several different angles trying to get a better focus on the victim's face. She shook and dropped the book; tears welled up in her eyes.

"It's not Charles White, its Chaz or Whitey. He was a babysitter for my kids. Phil had been promoted to the Sergeants' Mess and Chaz was one of the young lads in the platoon that came round to mind the..." She stopped mid-sentence, overcome with emotion.

Janet couldn't believe the situation. It was the first time she had witnessed her analyst ever show any emotion about a case. All through a recent case against a man who had murdered his wife and three young children she had never shown the slightest hint of feelings.

"Have you got Buster's number? I'd better break the bad news to him."

Ordsall Estate, Salford

Buster was walking back to his car carrying his Subway bag when his phone rang. It was an unknown number.

"Hello, Phil speaking."

"Buster Johnston, this is DCI Janet Wood speaking from Syndicate Two FMIT. Are you free to talk?"

He recalled the pretty blonde Chief Inspector sitting at the front of a recent briefing about the capabilities of the surveillance team and technical unit. Her pale blue eyes almost distracted him from his topic.

"Afternoon, Ma'am. I'm just getting my dinner, but I need to get back on plot soon as we are on a live job."

Being the team leader Phil always waited until all the members of his team had taken time out to grab lunch before he went. He was also a stickler that the 'Refs' - refreshment break - was done quickly in case the subject of the day's surveillance decided to move.

"OK, I'll be quick," she started.

"I've been talking to your ex, Sharon."

"Oh, what has she been saying about me?" he interrupted. He seemed vexed at the mention of her name.

"Nothing bad, but she recognised an army pin badge on a murder victim, and she said you were in the same unit," she explained.

There was a pause before he answered.

"Which unit and who's the victim?"

"Fusiliers, Charles White, but Sharon told me that you knew him as Whitey or Chaz. He was a babysitter for your children."

Buster thought about his former companions.

Before he had left the Battalion he had been assigned as Two Platoon Sergeant in A Company. The unit was training to re-deploy to Northern Ireland and due to a lack of officers coming from Sandhurst he had stepped up to lead the platoon.

White was a young Fusilier, good head on his shoulders and was destined to have a good career in the army.

The lad had just turned eighteen when Johnston had taken command of Two Platoon. He was always at the front during the physical beastings dished out by his leader. A dependable young man that relished army life.

"Yes, I remember him. He was a decent soldier. Sharon's right, he did babysit our kids a few times before I left the Battalion."

"Why did you leave your regiment?" she asked.

"I had previously been seconded to a military surveillance team. I really shouldn't have gone back over the water, but the work was good. Somebody saw me and requested I return to special duties. What's the circumstances, Boss?" he enquired.

"Well, his throat was sliced, and we can't find any motive at the moment. He was happily married and semi-retired, even at his young age, due to his wife's family setting them up financially. No sign of robbery, his wallet was still in his coat pocket. No indication that it was due to a love interest on either side, and he didn't have any defence wounds, so the murderer got up close and attacked quickly."

"Or he knew his assailant," Buster added.

"It's a possibility which we are looking into."

"Look, Boss, I knew Whitey many years ago and it was only for a few months, so I don't know if there's much I can add to your investigation. I need to get back on plot with my team, but if I think of anything I'll give you a bell."

He finished his call and immediately scrolled through his phone book until he found the name Screech. He hit the call button and waited. Almost immediately a women's voice told him that the recipient was not available and advised on leaving a message.

"Jock, Johnno here. Give me a bell back. I need to ask you something."

He could imagine his Scottish friend in his blue scrubs pushing another patient into the operating theatre at Manchester Royal Infirmary.

Tom 'Jock' Bone was the only member of his old Fusilier Platoon that he stayed connected with. A fiery force of nature who played the bad guy Platoon Sergeant, compared to Johnston's 'good guy' Platoon Commander.

He had been given the nickname Screech behind his back by the troops because when he lost his rag he would screech at the top of his voice.

Sandwich Road, Eccles

The tall gangly man woke up sweating. He was pale and painfully slim. His stomach ached. Cancer, he was sure of it. The doctors were fucking useless, fobbing him off, just prescribing Gaviscon for acid reflux.

He knew it was cancer - or a huge ulcer eating through his guts.

The Army had caused it, out of date rations, training in nuclear, biological, and chemical environments, then the constant inoculations had taken their toll on his body. The doctors were covering it up, a conspiracy so the MOD could abandoned its duty of care.

He walked to the bathroom to see if the blood had soaked out of his black hoody. His mate had told him to burn everything after he did an operation, but he didn't have the money to throw about like him.

A mobile phone on the bedside table began to purr, the name Dovey appeared on the screen.

It was the only number in the cheap Nokia burner phone which had been handed to him by his one and solitary friend.

He snatched it up, pressed the green button and listened carefully to his instructions.

After putting the phone down, he opened a laptop lid and started looking at Google maps. 'Gorton', he typed into the request bar, then began to scroll.

Once happy with the location he trawled through Facebook and began noting the pictures of men attending an event in Manchester. He had found his next target.

Firs Flash Nature Reserve

Johnston was sweating as he scrambled to the top of the hill. It had been raining and the slope was wet and sticky with grey silicon mud which had been bulldozed into place many years before as coal spoil heaps from the long-gone coal mines that used to dominate the local economy and skyline.

Now the shale and carboniferous sandstone had been landscaped with trees and bushes.

The heaps were made from the material removed from the tunnels dug deep underground and they were an excellent training venue for the ex-soldier.

He reached up on to his shoulder strap tighteners and pulled and bowed at the same time, expertly moving the heavy Bergan higher up on to his back and shoulders.

After using the green straw of his water-filled camel pack, he viewed the scenery.

The industrial landscape of the past had been changed both by man and Mother Nature as old factories had been replaced by housing estates and the mines reclaimed by woods and forests.

His knee began to vibrate, his phone bleeped.

"Hello," he gasped.

"Johnno, it's Tom. How you do', mucker?" the Scottish voice asked.

Tom Bone was his usual bright self. No matter the darkest of situations Jock would be jovial, unless he was screaming at the men under his command.

"Thomas." Johnno smiled as he spoke, speaking to his former sidekick always cheered him up.

"Have you heard about Whitey being murdered? He had his throat cut up at a country park in Bolton," Johnno explained.

"I heard, aye, it was on the local news. He was a good man; his wife's family are loaded. They own a battery company and are making money hand over fist because of this move to electrify anything with wheels. I had a pint with him at the last Fusilier Re Org."

"What's the Fusilier Re Org?" Johnno asked, puzzled.

Ten years before a group of Fusiliers had attended a funeral for a dear comrade. Over a beer or ten they had come to the drunken conclusion that the only time they had got together were funerals or the mandatory Remembrance Day.

Within weeks they had organised a get together in Manchester which they named the Fusilier Re Org! as in reorganisation. Over the years the gathering had grown from the first meeting of twenty-nine to the present-day figures of one hundred and fifty.

Soldiers who were from corps attached to the Fusiliers now attended with wives and Fusilier children. It was a good excuse to reunite, tell war stories, unload problems, and get rat-arsed.

"Agh, you need to come, Johnno, it's a great bash at the Rain Bar in town. Every year the blokes ask about you. They all tell war stories about the way you led the platoon in South Armagh and Coalisland. They also make up tales about where you disappeared to."

"And where did I disappear to?" Johnno asked.

Tom laughed down the phone. "Well, some say you were kicked out for screwing the CO's wife and others say it was the SAS."

"And what do you tell them, mate?"

"Johnno, I tell them the truth. I told them you came out and you're a barber in the Gay Village in Manchester," he chuckled.

"You're not far wrong, mate. I bet that raises a smile with the troops."

"Nah, they all know you were a top swordsman. You would shag any women that smiled at you, married or not."

Sergeant Phil Johnston was a philanderer, he couldn't keep his dick in his combats. NAAFI staff, nurses, civilian members of staff, female soldiers or colleagues' wives were all fair game. He was lucky with his constant adultery: he chose well, had a good memory and the luck of the devil.

Only once had he almost been caught on the job when a husband returned from a course unexpectedly, which led to Johnno shimmying down a well-placed water pipe to escape from the flat he was trapped in.

He didn't look back on his conquests with any satisfaction. He didn't try to speculate or reflect why he did what he did. Subconsciously he believed it was a domination thing and possibly linked to his mother's alcoholism and prostitution.

As a youngster he had been present when his mum and her friends had been getting ready to go to 'work', so he viewed most women as objects to be conquered.

His first sexual experience had been with one of his mother's friends. After his first encounter word had soon spread that Vera's lad had the equipment and stamina. Soon the working girls were lining up to teach him the ways of the world.

"How's Caz?" he asked to try and break the vision in his head of the scores of women lying beneath on top of or beside him.

"Who, Caroline? Aye, she's fine. She stays connected with the wives' club. I swear they know more than we ever did. I'll ask her about Whitey as I bet, they've discussed it round the campfire."

"Around the witches' coven more like. Anyhow, who comes to this gathering?" he asked.

"Most of the old Two Platoon. They come from all over the world. Phil Powell flew in from LA one year. The Geordies come en masse and stay for the weekend. Some of the Brummies' and Coventry lads crash at the local lads' houses 'cos they are tight as fuck and the Cockneys are usually pissed by seven o'clock because they aren't used to real beer."

"So, most of our old Northern Ireland Platoon attend?"

"Yes, mate, and they want to see their old Platoon Commander. It wasn't the same when you handed over to Lieutenant Barnes and I was promoted and moved to C Company. At the end of the tour, they did a deployment to Belfast and were surrounded. Ratty, one of the young lads, was snatched and was missing for a few hours before the Secret Squirrels rescued him."

"Paul 'Ratty' Rattigan, tall skinny kid in Anderson's brick?"

"That's the guy, his head fell off after his rescue. He did a few years, but he was caught during a compulsory drugs test and booted out. I think they had moved him to the Officers' Mess as a waiter by then. He comes to the Re Org. I think he works locally, always asks about you."

The last time Johnno had seen Paul 'Ratty' Rattigan he was carrying his battered and bloody body out of a flat in Twinbrook, South Belfast. The young soldier was naked, his skinny body a mass of cuts, broken bones, burns and bruises.

After his abduction army and police handlers had been pushing their informants for news about the whereabouts of the missing soldier. Luckily, the information was timely and accurate, and the source well placed enough to stop any PIRA inquests pointing the finger at her for being an agent for the Crown Forces.

A team from the East Detachment of the Special Reconnaissance Unit and eight members of Ulster Troop Special Air Service Regiment had assembled and stormed the second floor flat.

The hostage was safely recovered, unlike his captors who had either been shot or died trying to jump from the balcony.

Johnno had started immediate first aid and administered a cannula and saline drip into Ratty who was barely conscious.

Even if he had have been aware of his saviours it was doubtful, he would have recognised that the man behind the balaclava treating his wounds was his former Platoon Commander.

"Did you hear about Winker? Don Watson, the Corporal who was in your multiple."

Johnno was trying to remember the old infantry patrolling concept.

Four men in a brick led by a senior Fusilier or Junior Non-Commissioned Officer and three or more bricks made a multiple which was commanded by a Senior Non-Commissioned Officer or full-blown Sandhurst trained Rupert.

Again, shame came to mind. Johnno remembered Don 'Winker' Watson well and his wife Donna, a petite stunning blonde with a risqué mouth.

He put the thrusting young Corporal on a multitude of career courses to 'help his career'. While Winker was away Johnno looked after his slim leggy wife, often meeting her at her sister's address in Newtownards.

Even after his move back to the SRU they carried on their affair. When Winker was away, she would find her way back to Johnno's bed.

"How is Winker? I heard he made it to CSM?"

"He became the Motor Transport Sergeant Major. He's disappeared, mate. He was due to come to the last gathering but never turned up. One of the lads saw him on the ferry coming over but he hasn't been seen again. Caz is still in touch with his wife, Donna. Her and the kids are devastated."

"Where's Donna now?"

"Aye, I knew you'd be asking that. When Winker got out, they settled in Crawfordsburn in Ireland. He was a driver for some fly-by-night agency, and she worked in a pharmacy."

"How did you know I'd ask about Donna?"

Tom was roaring with laughter.

"Have a look at her son and then try and tell me you weren't shagging her when Winker was away or on guard duty. Me and Caz went over to visit them both a few years ago. They have a beautiful bungalow on Burnside Park. I swear to God I nearly choked when Winker introduced me to 'his' son, Peter. He's your double. Come over for a brew and I'll get you up to speed with where the lads are at. Now Whitey's dead the next reunion might turn into a wake so it would be good to have you back with the crowd. Just tell them about your hairdressing job and it'll put them off boring you all night – well, apart from Strangler, who's come out of the closet."

"What, six-foot five Strangler? The Cockney monster is gay?"

"He's going the full transition, bless him. He said his pent-up anger was due to him being a woman in a man's body, so if he wants a kiss, you'd better pucker up."

Johnno dropped the phone back into his pocket and felt the familiar strain on his shoulders as he resumed his tab across the hills of his local beauty spot. The vision of Strangler in high heels, mini skirt and lipstick was emblazoned on his mind.

Hazelbank Park, Newtownabbey

The man with the limp handed over the ice cream cone to the older man sitting on the park bench. His eyes were fixed on a small cargo vessel slowly riding over the choppy waters towards Belfast Harbour.

He rested his stick at the side of the bench, then sat beside the other man.

"So, what's going on, Sir John? Why all the haste?"

The older man was dressed smartly in a pinstripe suit, crisp pink shirt, and a green, red, and yellow regimental tie. His shoes were highly polished.

He stroked the neatly groomed whiskers of his trimmed grey moustache.

Through the trees he could just make out the distinctive yellow shapes of Samson and Goliath which were the old cranes of the Harland and Wolff shipbuilders: a proud shipbuilding tradition long since gone. Symbols of Belfast's industrial heritage, with one hundred- and forty-metre spans.

"I need you to move your ladies from the knocking shops you've created in the Rathcoole flats," he said, still looking towards the yellow cranes.

"What, do you realise how much money I have invested in those businesses?"

The old man looked at him incredulously.

"Look, Mr Charlton, the cash you make from your seedy little brothels will pale into insignificance when I give you a few titbits from the latest Belfast regeneration meeting I've just attended."

Charlton sat rebuked. For the next twenty minutes he listened to the old man talk about future developments. There was money to be made, lots of money. He felt his cheeks flush, and he smiled.

"The fuckin' Taigs won't play ball on the other project, Sir John. I tried to persuade Sean McGivern, a senior Provo, to start a bit of unrest by the peace line but he fucked me off."

"Well, you had better start getting creative with the assets you have at hand. Put your little fella from Birmingham on it. I need to get justification to get a bigger police budget and you need them to be dealing with the Catholics whilst you build up your business."

Highbank Estate, Gorton

Del Anderson parked his red Post Office van on the bend on Tannery Way in Gorton. He carefully backed into the parking space before retrieving a small red bag with the M18 8LH postcode stencilled on top.

Behind the van the line of trees hid Gorton Lower Reservoir and the Fallowfield Loop footpath.

One final bag and the estate delivery would be complete. It would then be back to the depot and a quick brew before starting the parcel deliveries.

He hated deliveries to this estate, new Noddy houses, no soul, the locals were all up their own arses and didn't give him any time or notice. No interaction or people skills.

He much preferred the old estates off Mount Road. The occasional brew stops, talking to pensioners who appreciated his service and having some banter with the street scallies, who kicked a ball around in the street.

The tall gangly man stepped back from the tree line and waited. He had parked his mountain bike by the trees on Gore Brook then made his way towards the new estate. He had only been waiting a few minutes when the red van turned up and parked directly in front him.

The smell of diesel fumes was in his nostrils. He immediately recognised the postman as he unlocked the back door of the van. Skinny hairy legs, long limbs, shiny bald head, and ever-present sneering smile.

Years of pent-up frustration surged through his veins. Whitey had never given him any hassle after the incident whereas Big Del had been one of his main tormentors. Anderson and the new Platoon Sergeant made his life a living hell.

Anderson was no friend of his. After the incident he took pleasure in taking the piss out of his new stammer. Ridiculing him in front of new members of the platoon, he might have been a senior Fusilier with a wealth of experience, but the gangly man hated him with a passion.

Murdering Whitey had upset him - he cried as he cleaned his blood off the karambit. Whitey was always decent with him and never joined in with the banter, Dovey had told him that his old comrades knew where the prize was and if he found the prize their backer would pay for a top surgeon to remove the cancers and tumours eating away at his guts.

Dovey wanted questions to be answered, but this time it was personal.

He knew that it wouldn't take long for his target to complete his task in the cul-de-sac. He had watched him on three separate occasions, shaking with rage as he did so.

Most of the street were out at work and the local dog walkers were back home having a brew and watching 'Homes Under the Hammer'.

He heard Anderson whistling as he walked back down the slope to the waiting van.

His hood was now pulled up and the blade held tightly in his hand. The postman pulled out a sweet from the cargo pocket of his issued shorts and greedily shoved it into his mouth. He threw the wrapper on to the road as he sauntered along.

The rear doors of the van made a squeaking sound as he fully opened them. He looked at the now-empty van apart from the flat bags which he had already delivered.

The gangly man stepped out of the wood line and through the walkers' gap in the wooden fence. He walked around the back of the van and could smell the stench of new piss as Anderson relieved himself on to the grass.

He looked left and right, keeping himself close to the van as he pissed.

The man grabbed the back of Anderson's neck and kicked him behind the knee, pushing him down to the now-warm wet grass.

"What the fuck…!" he screamed in surprise.

The standing man placed his foot on the centre of the postman's back, pushing him deeper into the steaming wet turf.

"Tell me where Johnno is?"

"Go fuck yourself, you prick! There's nothing in the van, no credit cards. You're late, you fucking smack head!" he shouted defiantly.

The gangly man dropped with all his force until his knee hit the centre of the prone man's spine.

"You always were a bully, Anderson. Now tell me where Sergeant Phil Johnston is, or I'll cut your ears off."

The prone man yelped as the bony knee dug into the small of his back. It took his breath away, his mind was swirling, but the voice was familiar - then it hit him like a lightning bolt.

"Is that you, fuckin' bed wetter? Burbling fucking nonce, do you want to run to the Sarge and start crying on his shoulder like you used to do in Ireland, you fucking red arseeeee!"

"AGHHH!"

CHAPTER THREE

Ashton-in-Makerfield

The small bathroom under the stairs was spotlessly tidy - he was in a well maintained and scrupulously cleaned home.

The two Scottish terriers that had growled and moaned until he stroked their bellies were also well groomed and well-manicured, apart from the occasional beefy fart, which made Caroline dash for an air freshener.

Caroline and Tom were made for each other. She tall, blonde haired and blue-eyed English rose, and him a small slim greying Scotsman with bowlegs. Johnno always teased them that he didn't believe in mixed marriages and Arian beauties should not be marrying porridge gobbling barbarians.

The toilet was the only place you found anything to commemorate Tom's military service. Pictures, certificates, and mementos covered the lilac walls.

He looked at a picture of a group of men standing on an armoured vehicle in front of a silver wriggly tin wall.

Outside there was a cry: "Oh noooo!" The old firm game was on, and Tom's side had gone behind.

Slowly he scanned the line of young faces, recalling them name by name: Corporal Watson, Ferguson, Miller, Gaught, Abbott, White, Anderson, Smith 55, Smith 19, Jones 98, Dove, Rattigan, were the ones he recognised immediately. One or two faces he struggled to name. Tom was in the middle, dwarfed by the rest of the platoon, whilst Johnno was sitting smiling on top of the green armoured car, the only one not wearing any headdress.

He caught Caroline clearing up the dishes in the kitchen.

"Which is Tom's favourite dog, Caz?" he asked with a cheeky grin.

She smiled and pointed to Hamish. Johnno quickly retreated to his hung-up coat and retrieved an item before re-joining Tom.

Ow's and ooohs were being yelled as Tom kicked an imaginary ball. As well as playing he was also the ref and manager, shouting advice to the Rangers manager hundreds of miles away. His team were now two goals down against their opponents wearing green and white hooped shirts.

A man wearing a blue shirt burst through the defence and then proceeded to hit the ball high over the bar. Tom then commenced coaching the player on how to kick a ball into a goal.

"Fuck me Tom that balls just landed in your back garden." Phil teased.

Tom was in mid-flow talking to the television set when he was distracted by something scuttling towards him on the floor.

"Ach noooo, what have ya done to ma wain?"

The little Scotty pawed at her master for attention, proudly sporting a green and white scarf around its neck.

"Poor Hamish, I'm going to have to scrub him to get that shite off his fur."

He turned to Phil and the laughing Caroline who was now standing in the doorway.

"Caz, how could you let him defile my wain like that?" He moaned.

Before he could say another word there was a roar from the TV and Tom looked to see a group of men in hoops hugging each other again.

Highbank Estate, Gorton

DCI Wood approached the red Post Office van, its rear doors covered by a white tent. She wasn't sure if it was the same one, she had been in up at the Jumbles murder: if not it was an exact copy. Perhaps the GMP forensics unit bought a job lot of them to prevent cross contamination. The sun was at its zenith, beaming. She had needed the air conditioning on during her drive to Gorton.

"You're going to need a mask on, Boss. The body has been in the van a while and it's quite ripe in there."

She turned round to see Griz, the principle SOCO. The hood of his white forensic suit was down, and his mask was over his throat. He was taking large gulps from a bottle of water.

"Frenzied attack on a postman. Attack occurred outside the van then the body put inside, possibly for concealment. There are droplets of blood leading back towards the gap in the fence, then tracks through the wood. I've got moulds of the footwear, but no fingerprints so far."

He fumbled in a bag and retrieved a plastic evidence container. She couldn't make out what was in it.

"What's that?" she asked.

"The victim's ears. He won't be wearing glasses again," Griz joked.

She started fumbling with the disposable white J suit. Griz held his hand out and offered her a ball of cotton wool.

"You might need this to shove up your nostrils. The body has been in the back of that van for a few hours, baking in the sun. It was only when the victim didn't turn up for his next delivery that they checked the GPS to find the van's location."

She opened the tent flap which allowed a dozen fat bluebottles to escape. There were two Scene of Crime Officers busy taking pictures and sifting through dry blood patches with needle-nose tweezers.

Beads of sweat instantly formed on her forehead. The stench of death seemed to seep in through her every exposed pore. The thick wads of cotton up her nostrils had little effect of keeping out the smell.

Unlike the Jumbles murder, this victim appeared to have been subjected to a frenzied attack. His body was covered with numerous slashes and stab wounds. His ears and nose were missing, and it appeared that the madman had tried to remove his quarry's eyes.

Laid out carefully on the van floor was a faded pink tongue.

"I'm no criminal psychologist, but in my layman's opinion I would say that this crackpot has wanted to take away the victim's senses. Sight, smell, taste, and hearing," Griz offered.

"Perhaps the removal of the tongue was a symbol of stopping him talking," Woods replied.

Rathcoole Estate, Carrickfergus

The woman was snoring beside him. She had stolen the quilt during the night, and he awoke shivering. Beside him one of his many mobile phones vibrated.

He cautiously peeked out of the window. Dirty white walls, some covered in Loyalist murals or graffiti, stared back at him. The estate was run down, gangs of idle youths stood blankly on the corner.

"Yes," he answered.

The voice was guttural broad Belfast, sentences littered with profanity and laced with threats.

"Look, he'll do it. I promise. He's not used to doing this work, but he knows who to look for."

More abuse emanated from the handset.

"Yes, I know I owe you and I'll sort this out. I just need a little more time. There's a gathering coming up soon and he might attend."

The line went dead.

He was no longer cold; he was dripping in nervous sweat.

Fuck! He cursed under his breath. His man on the mainland fucked up again, he was too highly strung, too many grudges to bear.

Only one job to do and he'd fucked it up by killing the man he was supposed to question. Just one simple question: where is Phil Johnston?

He had given him all the details; he had personally found Anderson on Facebook and friended him. Noted that he was a postman, even found his fuckin' round - what more could he do apart from torture the big fucker himself?

Bullcroft Drive, Astley

Buster put his arm around the proud young man.

"For a first car it's a cracker, lad."

The new car owner was beaming. "Thanks for sorting out the insurance, Dad."

"You owe me a pint. When you're old enough, of course," Buster jested.

The conversation stopped as a blue Ford Focus pulled on to the drive.

Buster's jovial mood suddenly changed.

"Hi, Mum, I'm on the road! Dad has sorted my insurance out."

Sharon seemed far from impressed.

She stared at her ex-husband. She appeared tired.

"What have I done now?" he questioned.

"Jamie, go and get the kettle on and make your dad a brew. I need to talk to him."

Both father and son looked puzzled. She waited until the lad had disappeared inside before she spoke.

"Now what do you want to argue about?"

"It's not about you, for a change, it's work. Our syndicate has just got another incident, a murder. Slashed to death. The attack almost severed the victim's head." She spoke slowly, trying to embed every word into his brain.

"And why do I need to know this?"

"The victim is Del Anderson. He was one of your lads in Ireland, just like Charlie White, wasn't he?"

Buster looked puzzled.

"Big Del, yes, he was one of my senior blokes. Real Jack the Lad, bit of a bully, so I had to rein him in a few times. He was a big unit. Why would somebody want to kill him?"

"Perhaps he was bullying the wrong people. He was a postie, but we know that no mail bags are missing so it's not a robbery. We're sure he's the target and seeing he was in the same Battalion as the also deceased Mr White we are investigating the links between both murders."

He looked away; in the corner of the road a neighbour was peering through the window.

"The neighbourhood watch is on the ball, I see," he commented.

"Sharon, it's more than a coincidence. They were in the same platoon for a while." He thought for a while.

"I was talking to Jock the other night. He told me that Don Watson disappeared on a visit over here."

Her eyes narrowed. "Donna's husband, the husband of that slut you were fucking while we were married?"

"Look, the lad got on a ferry in Larne and never got off on the other side. It might be worth looking at."

"I take it if I find out anything you will be on the first flight over to console the grieving widow."

"Put your professional head on for once. I'm telling you, two good men are dead, a third one is missing. All served in the same platoon on an operational tour of Northern Ireland. Look at what they did over there, the incidents, who did they upset. I'll go back and get the names of everybody that served with them."

"Bastard!" she spat.

"Tell Jamie I can't stop for the brew." He quickly jumped into his car and sped off.

He scrolled through the phone book and hit the green call button on the dashboard.

"Jock, I need to see you again ASAP. Bring that platoon photo and get me Donna's address."

Fort Whiterock, Belfast, March 1998

Pat Scott stood at the back of the dark briefing room. The walls were illuminated by strip lights which were covered in maps of the local area and mug shots of all the local Provisional Irish Republican Army suspects.

Pat's green t-shirt with the sleeves removed was two sizes too small, but it showed off his chiseled abs and huge biceps which he flexed constantly. BEAST was emblazoned across his chest.

He surveyed his troops as they listened to the intelligence briefing being given by a Corporal from the local intelligence cell.

It was supposed to be a short two-week deployment from their base on the coast at Ballykinler to West Belfast to cover the changeover of the six-month infantry battalion.

They were the duty company and each platoon had been designated a camp in Belfast to patrol from whilst the new unit took over and settled in.

Everyone suspected that the incoming unit would be the last soldiers deployed to Belfast after thirty bloody years of the troubles.

Almost three and a half thousand dead and almost forty-eight thousand wounded on all sides. Men, women, and children - the bombs and bullets made no exceptions.

Peace was on the horizon: there had been daily demonstrations supporting a ceasefire. The city was split between those supporting the political situation and the dissidents who remained defiant to the last.

"There'll be a large 'Brits Out' protest on the Falls Road this afternoon whilst you're out on patrol. There is a complete out of bounds box en route so we just want you to monitor people attending from the Turf Lodge and the Ballymurphy estates. Try and give us some feedback as to what the attitudes are towards the peace process," the Corporal requested.

Scott wasn't taking in any of the briefing, flicking the ears of his soldiers sitting in the back row trying to take notes, or shouting at the guys at the front.

"Fuckin' wake up, Anderson, and ye two - White and Rattigan - you're in the gym with me when we get back in, I'm ganna knack both of ya's."

Scott had recently taken over as the Platoon Sergeant after being away at the training depot for two years. He had replaced the gregarious Tom Bone who had been promoted and posted to another company.

The Platoon Commander had also changed with a real-life Rupert Lieutenant Barnes taking over from the recently disappeared, but well liked, Sergeant Phil Johnston.

The new platoon staff were nothing like the old team. One was new, inexperienced, and cajoled by the other: a bullying menace who was subject to huge mood swings and liable to kick off at any moment.

Twenty minutes later the fourteen-man multiple was outside the large protective silver fence of Fort Whiterock, moving cautiously along the streets of Ballymurphy and heading slowly east towards Briton Drive.

"One One, I'm now at the edge of the out of bounds area. Lots of locals on their way to the parade, seems friendly enough," Corporal Watson informed his commander on the radio.

"Push down into the Rocks. Have a look if you can see any players hanging around," Scott ordered.

The terraced streets which lined the hill down to the Falls Road was known as The Rocks. On the corner of one of the streets sat the Rock Bar, a notorious flashpoint. The area was interlaced with back streets and rat runs, enabling the locals to pop up in front or behind any unsuspecting patrol. Especially soldiers that were new to the area.

"Scotty, that's in the out of bounds box, we can't go in, mate," Winker reminded him.

"Two things, Wanker Watson: I'm the fuckin' boss, tellin' ye to gan in, yah soft twat, and second - am not your fuckin' mate. Now get moving before I put a boot up your arse."

Reluctantly Watson obeyed.

Ten minutes later the whole multiple had been encircled on three different streets and was being forced down towards the main protest moving from the Clonards towards Andersonstown.

Scott was loving the melee, punching and headbutting anybody in his wake like a demented bouncer.

Only when they had received extra support from the Quick Reaction Force and managed to battle their way back to Beechview Park did Lance Corporal Walpole realise that one of his men, Rattigan, was missing.

Sean McGivern was standing behind the speaking dais in Falls Park awaiting the marchers and guest speakers to arrive.

His marshals had reported no trouble with the procession, but he was getting word that a group of dissidents who had been earlier turned away had vented their anger on a British army patrol.

He chuckled to himself. One last Brit-bashing before they all run off home, he thought.
A woman approached him, she was stern faced.

"Sean, we have a problem which might just put the whole peace process in jeopardy."

"What's the problem, Ma?"

"Those fucking eejit dissidents have snatched a soldier. I want him back in one piece, do you understand me? I don't care how many pieces those fuckers are in."

Within an hour somebody had rung the confidential hotline with details about a phone number and the possible hiding place of the kidnapped soldier.

Boundary Way, Belfast

Claire Flusk was three cars behind the black Range Rover she was following.

"That's a right, right, right on to North Boundary Street towards the subject address," she commentated.

It had been a busy morning tracking the vehicle to a meeting with other drug dealers on the Ballybean estate to the east of the city. The journey had been littered with stops at the bookmakers, bar, and a check on his interests at the brothel above the café on the Comber Road.

The amount of time he had spent there it was probable that the guy was sampling the produce.

She wondered how the ultra conservatives of Dundonald would react when they found out about the knocking shop in the heart of their neighbourhood.

Judging by some of the clientele in and out of the establishment it was probable that the morality of the area had somewhat nosedived.

It made all the team smile when the observer described a clergyman exiting the property, adjusting his dog collar as he closed the door behind him.

'I'm sexy and I know it' ringtone started emanating from her mobile. She giggled as she immediately recognised who was calling.

"Johnno, long time since you called. I take it you want something," she teased.

"Only you, my love. I'm planning on a trip over the water, and I need to hook up," he explained.

"So, what do you want, my body or my brain?"

"A bit of both in equal measure, to be honest. An old army colleague of mine went missing off a ferry a few months ago. I don't know the full circs, so I..."

"So, what you're really asking is that you want to put my job in jeopardy just to find out something for you. That's what you really mean, isn't it."

"Flusky, it's just a small enquiry, just find out who the officer in charge of the case is and I'll call them myself."

He knew she was mocking him, which he didn't mind. She was one of his star pupils, a natural surveillance officer. She fit into any environment she worked in, a complete grey woman when walking down a street.

A chameleon. With a brush of her hair, she could change from a smack head looking for a fix to a mother doing a school run or an estate agent on her way to complete a viewing.

He had seen her in gym kit and when made up to attend one of the many course piss-ups.

Her long brown hair had a shine and usually brushed her shoulders. She had a slim face with deep brown eyes which were exaggerated by natural long lashes.

"If I'm going to risk my job it's going to cost you, Phillip Johnston."

"Just name your price, my love." He was thinking about her firm shapely arse and the tantalising rose tattoo on her thigh which was always tantalisingly flashed when she wore short skirts.

She agreed to pick him up from when he flew in and took the details of his missing friend, Donald Watson, to do a little digging. What the hell, she thought - it'll be worth a good night out on the town, and he was always good for the craic.

Asda superstore, Alan Turing Way, Manchester

"Fuck me, Tom, re-printing that picture has cost me an arm and a leg."

Tom smiled. "And you call me a tight arse Scotsman! You'll claim it back on your next expenses no doubt. Stop whining and get your brew."

They sat side by side, pointing to each face and annotating a name to each one.

Corporal Watson was missing and White and Anderson were dead and still waiting to be buried.

Tom told his former Platoon Commander that the likeable Lance Corporal Eddie Walpole had died in a terrible industrial accident when an ISO container fell on him at the Port of Salford, a huge new export park set on the bank of the Manchester Ship Canal.

Paul 'Ratty' Rattigan, the kid captured by the IRA, also worked at the same port, but as far as he knew was not present when the tragedy occurred.

"Young Ratty is a bit of a bad luck charm. How did we survive our South Armagh deployment with him in the platoon?" Johnno joked, then pointed to the next face in the ranks.

"You'll remember Dove - Brummie, cocky little bastard," Tom said.

"Good soldier as I remember though. Quite a fit lad. I think he was a student on the last sniper cadre I took before I went back to the Det."

"Aye, that's the boy, but he left under a cloud. He went to another platoon, and it was believed he stole a 9mm pistol and ammo. It was never proved of course, but the head shed kept a close eye on his lifestyle. RMP Serious Investigation Branch were crawling all over him and his finances, so he left. The duty rumour was he shacked up with some bird from Newtownards who was related to the paramilitaries."

Johnno's phone rang. He looked at the screen and smiled. It said 'Blue Eyes'.

"DCI Wood, how can I help you, Ma'am."

As a civilian he didn't have to use the officer's title, but it was an unbreakable habit he had carried over from the military. In his eyes they wore the rank. If they deserved, it or not was another matter. For his last few years on the covert side of the British army the commissioned officers were just referred to as Boss whilst on duty and first names or nicknames when not.

He had been relaxed about rank policy in Two Platoon. Most of the troops referred to him as Johnno until Corporal Bone entered the room and gave them an earbashing about rank having its privileges.

Not long after taking over Two Platoon his Company Sergeant Major Abby Forest had taken him to one side as he was worried about the discipline.

"Sergeant J, these men are not your old chums in the Special Forces. They'll fuck up and let you down. Just remember, familiarity breeds contempt."

Abby was a big man, former Army heavyweight boxing champion, always the smartest man on parade, whereas Johnno only looked smart in his camouflaged ghillie suit. Being smart and tidy was an occupational hazard to a man who preferred to do his soldering in the fields rather than the barrack room.

He heeded his Sergeant Major's sound advice as Abby was the consummate professional.

"May I call you Buster?" she enquired.

He smiled and told her that was fine. It was usually just members of his surveillance team that used his handle.

"Sharon has just mentioned at our morning meeting that there is another man from your unit that has gone missing, and you are going to visit Northern Ireland to speak to his relatives."

There was a long pause as the DCI quickly thought of an action plan.

"Your information is correct, Boss, but I don't know the circumstances or the exact date he went missing."

"Look, Buster, my team are struggling with our case files and a tight budget. I know you will be on leave, but it would be much appreciated if you could do a little digging and maybe submit a statement with your findings. If you find anything I can then justify a trip over for one of my officers to do some further research."

"No problems. I'll see what I can dig up."

"I can probably stretch my budget to pay for a few expenses but nothing too extravagant, and I am aware that you are quite close to the two victims of our murder enquiry so please beware of the conflict of interests which any subsequent trial could use to undermine our case. Please tread gently," she asked.

"No footprints in the sand, I understand. You might want to look at another strange death. Eddie Walpole, former member of the same platoon. He had an ISO container drop on his head at the Port of Salford. It's down as an industrial accident, but..."

"But you think it's worth examining?"

"Might be nothing, but when you put it all together you never know. Ciao."

He ran his fingers through his hair and pondered whether he needed a haircut. Tom looked at him with a questioning look.

"I'm off to Belfast, mate, but strictly information gathering. Will you ask Caz to ring Donna? I don't want her to have a heart attack when I turn up on her door."

Tom had a beaming smile.

"You'd better prepare yourself for your own heart attack when you see her wain."

Cupar Way, Belfast

There were around a hundred men in the procession and quite a few children acting as spotters. The mood had been quite jovial until they had reached the police barrier at North Howard Street. Balaclavas and masks were now being used to conceal identities.

Most of the marchers had been bussed in to the area from South East Antrim and left in the local pubs on the Shankill to get plenty of bravery juice down their necks before starting the Protestant Anti Papist march which was a protest about the attempts by Sinn Fein to replace the Union flags with the Tricolour throughout Belfast on certain days.

Somebody had decided that the target of the protest would be the Irish Republican History Museum. The problem was that the museum was in the Nationalist Clonard district and protected by a stone and brick twenty-foot peace wall. The wall had been a blank canvas for graffiti artists over the years and had become quite a tourist attraction.

The gates which allowed daily access were opened and closed by PSNI Officers in the morning then closed in the evening. These access routes quickly became a bone of contention and were flash points.

They could also be closed or manned if the tensions on either side rose above the norm.

A smell of booze was prominent on the assembled, many of which had been ordered to attend or face the consequences. A large fine or a beating would be dished out for any dissension in the ranks of the Loyalists.

Behind the locked steel barriers was a line of police officers wearing black helmets, visors down, looking aggressive; behind them white police vehicles with a larger group of Officers carrying riot shields lay in wait. The march came to a halt and the insults began.

Ross Road, Belfast

The house had been carefully chosen due to its view. The small window at the rear of the property was tiny but gave an excellent view along North Howard Street and the disturbance taking place by the barrier.

A few bottles had been thrown and the police commander on the ground had sent his shield-carrying troops forward to support the line.

Downstairs in the house a terrified young couple lay bound and gagged on the kitchen floor. A man with a scarf over his face sat above them pointing a pistol at their backs.

Upstairs the sniper made a few adjustments to the telescopic rifle. He scanned the crowd for his target: white baseball cap and carrying a placard. Two hundred and ten metres he had estimated, and then checked on an app on his phone. He began to regulate his breathing and watch the rise and fall of the cross hairs in the sight.

The sniper identified the man John Bushell from Greenisland, a family man who was on the march to pay off a loan debt but had got behind on his repayments. He had been told on the bus down to wear the white hat to identify himself as a civilian, unlike the fully fledged UVF members that were up for a fight.

Bushell was standing towards the rear of the mob. He stood out because no one stood with him. A loner, Billy no mates - then his head exploded.

Next day's tabloids ran full-page spreads about the innocent Protestant father of four shot dead by a Republican sniper whilst on a peaceful protest.

CHAPTER FOUR

Rain Bar, Manchester

Johnston had promised himself that he would be on the first purple bus back out to the sticks if he didn't know anyone at the Fusilier Re-Org. Judging by the noise and laughter emanating from within the party was in full swing.

"Are you with the old soldiers?" the barmaid asked.

"Many years ago, but I doubt if anyone will remember me," he confessed.

She poured him a Guinness with expertise and handed it over.

"Take a drink for yourself, love," he said as he offered his card to pay.

"My name is Sara, I'm the manageress. These nights get so busy that I'm all over the place. Behind the bar one minute and upstairs the next."

He chuckled "Upstairs? Well, I always said the Fusiliers were lovers not fighters."

She gave him a cheeky smile. "Eh, none of that goes on in here. We're a respectable establishment, I'll have you know! Upstairs is our second bar and the buffet." She then winked at him.

I've not lost it, he told himself. He prided himself on his success with women.

She was cute, small, brown bobbed hair and bright green eyes, maybe he would stay on a little even if he didn't know anyone. He lifted the cold bitter liquid to his lips when a big black hand rested on his shoulder.

He noticed a Fusilier plaque behind the bar and 'Fusilier Ale' on one of the beer pumps.

"Johnno, you old bastard, it must have been twenty years since I last saw you."

The black man was a bear of a human being, his head was shining - it looked like it had been buffed up for parade. His perfect teeth shone as he gave a huge smile. His wide mouth was underlined by a smartly trimmed grey goatee beard.

"Bertie? Bertie Reid? As I live and breathe!" He hugged on to the big guy.

After a few minutes' catch-up the big former Corporal ushered his protégé through the mass crowd and out of the back doors on to an outdoor terraced area.

Sets of high bar stools surrounded barrel tables which were all covered in glasses and bottles. Above each table was a large parasol and a heater. It was the end of a July's day in Manchester and clouds were beginning to hover above the party.

Johnno estimated about two hundred, maybe more, all chatting away. Some of the groups had navigated to the edge of the canal. He wondered who the first swimmer of the night would be.

An older guy was wandering around, going from table to table taking pictures. His face was familiar, but he couldn't put a name to him. The guy was very jovial and was having a crack with everyone, especially the wives.

"I'll be licking this picture tonight," he joked with one woman.

"Oh, put me in your next book, Jack!" the woman hysterically screamed.

"He writes porn stories in his spare time," Bertie explained.

Bertie introduced him to people, some of whom he knew well, others vaguely. He heard Tom before he saw him.

"Oh no, the Platoon Commander has finally graced us with his presence."

Tom put his arm over the new arrival's shoulder and propelled him towards a group of men all standing at the bottom of brickwork steps. They all had a beer in hand and were talking loudly. It looked like they had started the reunion much earlier in the day.

As he was propelled towards the waiting throng a dishevelled drunk stepped in their path and held out his hand.

"Johnno, good to see you again," he slurred. His eyes were bloodshot red, his body odour of ale and piss was alarming.

He was fat and stunk of stale sweat. His pupils were dilated as he shuffled from side to side.

"Fuck off, Scotty, and didanee come near our troops. They'll fuckin gub yah drunken basa!" Tom growled as he pushed Johnno past the alchy.

"Who the hell is that?" Buster was bewildered.

"Pat Scott, he was the Platoon Sergeant who took over from me. It was on his watch that the young lad Rattigan was snatched," he explained.

Back in the day Scott was a bodybuilder of some repute, but years of over training and niggling injuries led to his increasing use of steroids, then booze, as his figure transformed from Greek God to Buddhist effigy.

Johnno reached the veterans of Two Platoon and for thirty minutes shook hands, had his picture taken and was asked what he wanted to drink.

In the centre of the gathering was a long-legged blonde wearing a tight leather short dress showing off a more than ample amount of cleavage.

Phil tried to remember if he had met this woman before or if she was the wife of one of the troops. The blonde turned to greet the new arrival and thrust out a large well-manicured hand.

"Hiya Sarge." The voice was deep with a definite Sunderland accent.

"Oh, hiya Strangler, my how you've changed since carrying the GPMG all over South Armagh." Johnno stammered.

"Body of Baywatch, face of Crimewatch!" The huge blonde laughed. Everybody joined in too scared not to show amusement with a former Macum hardcase.

The main topic of conversation was the deaths of White and Anderson. Some were speculating that it was the work of an IRA hit team, others thought it was to do with a fracas in the NAAFI back in Ballykinler with the Paras training on the local ranges.

None were convinced that Walpole's 'accident' was just that, and all believed that Watson was probably dead as well.

Two of the lads were standing outside of the conversation.

He recognised the tall slim figure of Fusilier Paul 'Ratty' Rattigan. He had changed considerably since he had last seen him. Their last encounter was in a dirty junkie flat in South Belfast. The young man had been naked apart from a black hood over his head.

The young man's body was covered in burns and bruises; his fingers were deformed after being 're-arranged' with a hammer.

Beside Ratty and almost a foot shorter stood Dave Dove. Dove was stocky, powerfully built: his once bright blond hair was darker and spikey. He had been one of Johnno's pupils on a Sniper course.

There was no doubt the Dove was a good soldier: he was sharp on the uptake and fit, but there was something about his character that Johnno didn't like.

Dove wasn't a team player, he would use people, stir the pot to bring others down, spread rumours to discredit.

He was never brave enough to put his head above the parapet, but happy for the more outspoken members of the group to spout his words.

"Do you remember Ratty and Dovey?" Tom said as he introduced the two men.

They both appeared nervous in his presence. The tall man was trying to avoid eye contact whist Dove couldn't stop staring at his former instructor.

"Yes, I do remember these two reprobates. I seem to recall I replaced the ammunition you lost in South Armagh from the GPMG you were carrying, Ratty, which got you out of the shit and you, Mister Dove,

I signed you off to become a sniper. What are you doing now - hit man at Mothercare?"

Over a few drinks the two younger men shared their stories. Rattigan briefly said he had been abducted by the IRA but had been rescued by the SAS. His mental state was in tatters. He pointed over towards Pat Scott who was stumbling from table to table asking for a charity drink.

"That wanker left me to die." Ratty pointed to the drunk with unsteady scrawny fingers.

Dove appeared to be smiling as Ratty recounted the event.

Ratty then told them that he left the army and got a job down at the new Port of Salford with Walpole, who had been the victim of a tragic accident.

"Eddie used to climb on top of a container during his lunch break in summer. He loved his tan, 'bronzed Salford god' he used to say. One of the lads noticed he didn't clock off, so we did a search and found his hand. One of the lifters must have dropped a container on him whilst he sunbathed."

Johnno remembered Walpole: good lad a boxer hard as nails but slept like a log. Trying to wake him up in the morning or trying to get him out of a warm sleeping bag for stag was a mission in itself. It was surprising that the fork lift operator never heard the Salfordian's snoring.

Dove confessed that he had signed off from the army due to the Military Police hounding him about a stolen pistol and ammunition, which he denied strenuously. The guard commander who had almost completed twenty years of service had taken the rap and been reduced in rank.

Now Dove was living in Antrim and running a delivery company. His Brummie accent had developed an Irish twang and a few 'Ulsterisms' had crept into his vocabulary.

"Tom told us you were a cop, Johnno?" Dove asked.

Fuckin' Jock, Buster thought.

"Nah, I work for the old bill as a driving instructor. Boring really, lots of paperwork, but it pays the bills," he quickly answered.

"Wife and kids OK, Sarge?" Ratty asked.

It suddenly dawned on him that Ratty had once babysat his kids when his usual babysitter, Charlie White, was on leave. Sharon had fussed over the tall gangly kid, making him a pile of sandwiches, and even making him a brew when she came in pissed from the mess function.

"Gone, mate, we split years ago. I think she's down south now. I never hear from her or the kids. I just check my bank balance each month to see if she's still getting the CSA payments," he lied.

"You live in Manchester?" Dove asked for no apparent reason.

"Hey, it's my round, guys, what are you having?" Johnno asked and made his way to the bar.

As he stood waiting for the beer to be poured Johnno watched Rattigan and Dove in conversation. It appeared heated. Dove was the obvious alpha male in the pairing.

Dove broke away, then appeared with his back to another window. He was using a mobile and shaking his head. His appearance was now animated, as if he were giving orders to an impudent child.

"How's the party going?" Her Manchester accent was soft.

"Hi, Sarah. I'm a bit mesmerised by the whole event. I've been out seventeen years, so I'm really surprised how many people still remember me."

She had an inviting smile. "I'm sure that nobody would ever forget you," she teased.

"I'll try and make time to talk to you later. Once I've broken contact with these boring bastards," he joked.

He returned with the beer to Rattigan and Dove. They were whispering. The dynamics of the group had changed.

"Chorley," Buster said as he handed over the drinks.

"What?" Dove seemed confused.

"Before I got the drinks in you asked where I live and I'm telling you I live in Chorley, which reminds me I must check my train timings." He pulled out an orange ticket from his pocket and appeared to study the details.

The ticket was a prop he always carried when on foot. It was a handy tool when following somebody into a train or tram station. It made him appear to have a good reason to be in the premises.

"Didn't you tell us on the sniper course that you were born and raised around a mining village and honed your fieldcraft skills in the farmers' fields surrounding the pit?"

"I did, well remembered. Ellerbeck Colliery, south of the town. I still go running around there. Last train is at five to eleven, so I'd better mingle, guys. Good to catch up with you again." He inwardly sighed. Quick thinking on his feet and a good memory back to his school days and the project he did about the Lancashire coal mines.

His inner spider senses were tingling. The questions from the other guys were quite basic and not intimate unlike Dove's.

"Where do you get your train from? I might be going back to Brum tonight. You can show me the way to the station," Dove asked.

"The train I'm booked on is leaving from Victoria, Dovey, but you'll need to go from Piccadilly. If you're still about when I bug out, I'll point you in the right direction as they're opposite sides of the city, you know."

"Just give me your mobile number and you can text me when you're ready to leave."

Johnno smiled. "I'm a dinosaur, Dovey. I've left my phone at home to get recharged. When I go out, I don't like to be disturbed, but write your number down and I'll bell you when I get a chance."

"Just give me your number and I'll call you. When you get home the missed call will be me."

It was verbal jousting with neither man willing to divulge their contact details.

"It's a new phone, mate, I can't remember what my new number is." He shook hands with both men and walked away to find Tom.

"Quick selfie before you go, Johnno? I'll send it you," Dove asked.

He had run out of excuses so relented. "Yes, but get my best side," he joked.

He was annoyed with his Scottish friend.

"What were you thinking, telling those two muppets I work for the cops?"

"Arr, it's fine. They're just wains, trying to re-connect with their mates and people they respect."

Buster grabbed the slurring Scotsman by the arm and led him up to the buffet.

"Eating is cheating," the Jock protested.

Sarah was still smiling and arranging more plates and cutlery.

"Any chance you can sort out two coffees, please, love?"

"Ha-ha, the look on your face when you realised that the big blonde was Strangler was priceless." Tom said, giggling away in his drunken state.

"Look, Tom, we have members of our platoon dead on a cold slab in the mortuary, one man missing and a 'tragic accident' bullshit. Get your head on, man. The first thing you forget is operational security. During the present climate don't tell anybody anything about where you live, work or what car you drive."

"Why can't I give my number out? You're just jealous that the troops liked me more than you," Tom scoffed.

"It wasn't a popularity contest, Tom, and by the way you were a bastard with them. A good bastard, to be fair, but once a bastard always a…."

"OK, I get the message." Tom held up his hands as the coffee arrived.

"Just remember, modern phones are tracking devices. If somebody has your number, you're opening yourself up to a world of pain. Who's the guy taking photos of the event? They might be of use to the police."

"That's Jack Walters, he goes to every event. He can get where water can't."

He remembered Jack, former Corporal in C Company. A kind man who looked after the young lads when they arrived in the Battalion.

Johnno patted his friend on the shoulder and went to the buffet. He took a mental note about the unofficial photographer and promised himself to get his details for DCI Wood. He returned with a plate piled high with curry and rice.

"Eat and then drink your coffee and switch on."

Sarah was observing what was going on. "Is he going to be alright?" she asked.

"He's a happy drunk and he's a Jock so he's too tight to throw up and give away all the beer he's been drinking. I'll order him a cab once he's finished."

"Do you fancy a lock-in later?"

It was a great offer "How many are you considering locking in?"

"Just me and you. I've never seen you at the Fusilier Re Org night. It makes a change to be talking to somebody who's not pissed by now or looking at my cleavage."

"Sarah, it's an offer I can't refuse. I just need to check on something and I'll be back." He then went downstairs to the area overlooking the canal. Tom was still busy bulldozing his way through the curry.

The crowd had started thinning out, probably off to one of the multitudes of late-night clubs and drinking dens which had sprung up all over the city.

He looked into the main bar. Dove and Rattigan were standing at a high table intently watching the front door as people drifted off into the night. He retraced his steps back outside and made his way up the stairs only to find Tom had gone. His almost empty plate was about to be picked up by Sarah.

"Did you see where Tom went to?" he asked urgently.

"His exact words were, 'I've had enough hen, I'm off to my basha!' Then he went down the front stairs towards the toilets. It's not even chicken, it's lamb."

"No, Jocks use the word 'hen' like we say 'love'. They're just like Geordies with their heads bashed in."

She looked at him puzzled as he dashed off down the back stairs, leaving her holding the dirty plate.

Dove was still holding his view of the doorway; Rattigan was nowhere to be seen. The toilet was by the front door down a spiral staircase which left Johnno in a predicament. His friend might have been down in the toilet being attacked or fallen asleep on the porcelain with his trousers around his ankles. It wouldn't have been the first time either.

He ducked back outside and retrieved his mobile phone from his sock and switched off the in-flight mode and rang the Scotsman's number.

"Nee worry, mother. I'm on ma way to ma bus, laddie. Stop panicking."

Johnno was relieved that his friend was safe and heading away from the venue. Through the window he could still see Dove who was making a phone call himself, but this time he was using a smaller phone.

Rattigan had still not re-appeared; in his mind he reflected on the conversation he had had with Dove and his tall friend. They were more interested in his personal circumstances rather than past events. Every other group was swinging the lantern and telling past war stories, embellishing each tale as it was relayed.

It was more than suspicious, but perhaps explainable. Rattigan looked like he needed a crutch to unload his problems on and Dove was just a nosey bastard.

Rattigan had still not returned so he made his way down to the canal and followed the small pathway back towards the city. A metal fence which jutted out over the cold water was an obstacle but not a deterrent. He held on to the bars on one side and swung out over the cold dark water and around the cast iron overhang.

He then climbed a flight of wooden stairs and ducked through a passageway until he was out on to Great Bridgewater Street, walking towards the city. To his left punters were sitting on the benches outside the Peveril of The Peak. He saw two men standing by the wall facing across the road.

'Absence of the normal, presence of the abnormal,' a saying his grandad had drummed into his head before he joined the army.

One of the men spotted Johnno and looked at the screen on his phone, then showed the screen to his friend. They were like peas in a pod. Cropped hair, goatee beards, stud earrings, gold necklaces over tight black t-shirts. They may as well have had GANGSTER written across their large foreheads.

He tried not to give away the fact that he clocked them and walked away towards the McDonalds, putting on a shuffle as if he had had one too many.

McD's was busy with drunks with the munches, but he wasn't interested in food, only the CCTV inside. He waited in line to give them time to catch up, but they didn't take the bait, instead waiting outside by the stone-fronted Italian restaurant across the road.

After collecting his order of a burger and large Coke he smothered the food in tomato ketchup leaving the top of the bun off and made his way back out on to the street.

If his assumption was correct, they had his picture from the selfie and probably thought that he was going to stagger off in the direction of Piccadilly. Then again assumption was the mother of all fuck ups. They could be jealous husbands of women he had seduced or gang members that he had reported on.

He staggered towards the Novo Hotel on Portland Street then stopped, appearing breathless. People passed him and tried not to look at yet another drunk. Behind he could hear their footsteps approaching. He turned left into the darkness of the alcove.

"Are you OK, fella?" the first guy asked. His accent was broad Belfast, an Ulsterman no doubt.

Johnno was bent over as if he was about to spew. He took a quick glance at the foot placement of the men behind him. They were standing side by side, flat footed. The drunken man suddenly made a miraculous recovery. Spinning on his left foot he hit one guy in the eyes with the ketchup-covered burger then dispensed the sticky Coke into the face of the second.

A right hook to the chin put the first guy down and a stamp on the knee toppled the second. He turned and ran into the Novo Hotel then followed the signs through towards the NCP car park then out towards Manchester's bustling Gay Village.

After dropping back down to the canal towpath he jogged back to the Rain Bar. Sarah was at the backdoor about to close up.

"Is that lock in still available?" he asked.

She smiled and let him in to the now empty bar just as his phone began to ring.

"Hi, Tom, are you OK?"

"Thanks for the warning, I'm sober. I was walking towards the bus stop and thinking about what you said. I was sure I was being followed by a tall guy. He followed me on to a bus and went downstairs when I went up."

"What happened?"

"I jumped the bus two stops early and ran into my local park. I walk the dogs there, so I know it well. The guy got off, but he was probably too scared to come and follow me into the dark."

"Was it Ratty that followed you?"

"Tall enough, but I was still a little drunk, adrenaline running and all that so I couldn't put my hand on heart and say it was him. Do you think they have something to do with the murders?"

Johnno laughed. "You'd better ask my ex-missus, Tom. Sharon was always the best at coming out with conspiracy theories and jumping to conclusions."

"Aye, but she was normally correct."

Tom had a point.

Manchester City Centre

Sarah kissed him on the cheek as she opened the door to let him out. It had been a vigorous night and equally dynamic morning. The landlady had not had a boyfriend for a while and made up for it in one night. She also made an excellent breakfast.

He made his way to the alleyway of the Novo Hotel; the area was spotlessly clean after the work of the super-efficient Manchester Council street cleaners. He looked around and studied the positioning of the street cameras, then called Blue Eyes.

Nexus House, Ashton-under-Lyne

DCI Wood pressed pause on the recovered CCTV footage from the city centre cameras. They had watched Johnno carrying some items, then disappear into the arch leading towards the hotel. Moments later the two large men came into view and also disappeared. Ten minutes later the males staggered away towards a hire car parked on the NCP car park on an adjoining street.

The teams' detectives had worked fast. Two men, McClusky, and Freeman had left the car at Manchester Airport and departed on the same flight to Belfast as Dove. They neither sat nor checked in together. The CCTV from the airport showed that the guy calling himself McClusky had picked up a substantial limp during his trip.

The ID was probably phoney, but the CCTV from the incident and the airport had been sent to colleagues with the PSNI to identify just who McClusky and Freeman really were.

"Did you see any knives?" one of the detectives asked.

Johnno shook his head. "No, but I know this wasn't a random rolling a drunk on a Friday night gig. They were looking for me and if you ever get their phones, I'd bet they had a picture of me as well."

"Are you still happy to go over to Belfast?" the DCI asked.

"More than happy," he replied.

"My team spent the morning waking up your drunken former colleagues and have seized footage of the event. With that along and the CCTV from the bar we should be able to identify the person that followed your friend. Your friend Jack has done a wonderful job capturing everybody on film, including your whole Platoon."

"I'm more concerned with whoever they are. They now have an up-to-date picture of me."

CHAPTER FIVE

The Morning Star, Belfast City Centre

The early morning commuter flight from Manchester to George Best City Airport was only half full. A few business types and military personnel returning from leave, wearing expensive Fjällräven and Arc'teryx outdoor clothing.

During his era, he used to laugh at the Paras wearing their 'civilian' uniform of green bomber jackets, maroon t shirt, blue jeans, and desert boots.

After flashing his driver's licence at the waiting Ports Officer, he entered the large open plan arrivals lounge.

Claire was standing by the vending machines, her brown hair pulled back into a severe bun. Large, rimmed glasses accentuated the beauty of her deep brown eyes. She wore a tight pin stripped business suit and bright red high heels.

She held out her dainty hand to greet his arrival like a secretary picking up an important client for her boss.

"Follow me, Mr Johnston," she announced and led him out of the building towards the car park.

"Looking good, Flusky," he commented.

She smiled. "I'm in the big BMW executive car today so, as you always told us, I've dressed in the style of the car."

It was a good lesson to learn. Many operators had been compromised driving big expensive cars when looking like a penniless tramp or a hill walker.

Look the part on the street, in your vehicle, in the shop or at the pub. Look like you belong there, he had drummed in to all his students, even holding inspections before exercises to ensure they had disguises and backups.

'Street craft', he called it. He also used the morning's inspection as a chance to subtly assess each of the students' previous knowledge and worries about the course as the pressure of each exercise ramped up.

She dropped him outside his city centre hotel and disappeared to drop off the vehicle at a covert lock-up on the edge of the metropolis. An hour later she was changed into skinny jeans, her hair was down, glasses changed. She appeared to be a different woman.

They walked arm in arm along the bustling streets.

"Are you busy?" he enquired.

She laughed out loud. "C Branch are always busy, Phil. We've started picking up jobs from all over the place. There's a lot of unrest in the city at the moment. A sniper shot a guy on a protest the other week. Loyalists are claiming it was the Republicans and they're saying it was a set up. Up in Antrim the Prods are evicting anybody who's not a fan of King Billy, including Turkish barbers and Polish shopkeepers. It's manic."

Johnston had read the local papers on the flight over. Punishment beatings and shootings were on the up.

Masked men had been patrolling the streets, smashing shop windows, and firebombing houses. Settled asylum seekers were even considering returning back to their war-torn places of birth to escape the rising sectarian violence.

Any information that the police didn't know was usually revealed in the Sunday newspapers within a few days. Northern Ireland's investigative reporters were second to none. Regrettably many had been threatened or assaulted and a handful murdered.

Flusky led him to the black posts gateway of Pottingers Entry, an alleyway leading towards the Morning Star, a bar hiding between Ann Street and High Street.

The Morning Star was one of the oldest bars in Belfast. Green and gold paint frontage, the winged golden lion of St Mark dating from 1810 and Victorian signage grandly exuberant in its design gave the bar exhibited class.

The ex-soldier looked up at the large black iron brackets above the door and windows. It was an impressive place, and its exterior grandeur was matched inside by the original mahogany bar and terrazzo floor.

He ordered drinks and they took a place in one of the many secluded booths. As they took their first mouthful a man sidled over to them.

"Hi, Claire, I got here a bit early. Is this the friend you wanted me to meet? The name is Greg, Greg Tams. The disappearance of Mister Watson is one of my case load," he explained as he pushed himself beside Claire so he could face the new arrival.

Johnston was surprised. Claire had not mentioned any interlopers. He was also taken aback because the guy was not an Irishman.

Tams had been a Detective Sergeant in the Organised Crime Branch for many years after following his wife back to her home in Larne. He had transferred from Hampshire Constabulary after meeting Pam whilst she worked in the ferry port in Portsmouth. Now he was the owner of a small farm, tending goats and chickens.

The pace of operations in Organised Crime Bureau and the travel into the city had begun to take their toll so Greg moved out to the sticks and now ran the CID desk in the port town.

"From my office window I can look out towards the rolling Antrim hills and the arriving ships at the ferry terminal. I must admit that I daydream as I watch the rise and fall of the hungry seagulls as they swooped for food." Greg admitted.

He dealt with the occasional burglary, petty theft amongst the local farmers and the occasional assault amongst the town's drunks.

"How did you get allocated the crime?" Johnston asked.

"It's not a crime unless you can tell me something I don't know. It's a missing person who left via my local port, so I got the detail," he corrected.

He then told them that Watson was booked on to the European Causeway, a 20,800-ton ferry that could hold four hundred and ten passengers and three hundred and seventy-five cars which made the crossing to Stranraer in just two hours.

"Just over two hundred passengers got on and the same number of passengers and cars left so either somebody got on without being manifested or Watson got off in Scotland. Watson's car was never recovered. Fifty-five crew were interviewed. CCTV showed Watson in the Club Lounge. He ordered food and a hot drink, paid by credit card. Job done." Tams explained.

The Friday crossing had left on time at eight in the morning and landed at twelve o'clock with nothing unusual occurring.

Watson's car, a red Volvo estate left the ferry at Cairnryan, was never seen again. The registration tripped the ANPR camera leaving the port, and a photo was taken, but the windscreen was reflecting the sunlight so the driver couldn't be identified.

"Do you know if there were any paramilitaries on the ship that day?" Phil asked.

Greg put down his pint and appeared puzzled at the left-field question.

"The paramilitaries, why would they be involved? Do you think your friend had joined up?"

Phil looked around the bar, it had begun to fill up with dinner time customers.

Before he could answer Greg told him that the only name, he recognised on the manifest was a guy called Dove who was a former soldier and linked to the UVF in South East Antrim.

"Come to think of it there was also another former paramilitary I interviewed, Fat Tommy Taylor, as obstructive as ever. Dove was interviewed a few weeks later – TIE: Traced, Interviewed and Eliminated. He said he had seen him but travelled off on foot."

"They were both going to the same event so why didn't Dove get a lift with Winker Watson? It was just after mid-day when they landed, and the party started in Manchester at five?" he asked.

"Dove said he had made other arrangements and was going by train," Greg explained.

"What happened to the fat guy?"

Greg roared with laughter.

"That fat fucker has been disavowed due to being caught as a paedophile by 'The Manchester Hunters' an online group that sets up fake child profiles. They passed the information to your force who kindly disseminated it to PSNI. He's under investigation after we found indecent images on his computer. He's lost his job on the ferries."

"Would he know Dove?" Johnno questioned.

"Yes, there is CCTV of them talking on the ferry. They shake hands and then speak for a few minutes, then break up."

Johnno made a mental note to make a house call on Tommy Taylor.

"So do the Loyalist paramilitaries control Larne docks?"

The Detective's eyes narrowed as he looked at his inquisitor like he had asked an impudent question.

"No way. Yes, they transit the port, work there and even try and do the odd bit of smuggling, but they don't control it."

Johnno offered the Detective another drink which he readily accepted. He returned with his hands full of drinks and Tayto crisp packets.

"Has the MIR in Manchester been in touch yet?"

Greg gave him a stare. "Yeah, more actions to carry out on top of my creaking desk. I'll get round to answering their questions when I get time, and your DCI said she's sending one of her team over."

Johnno got the feeling that the Detective would not be happy with a member of the Manchester MIT looking over his shoulder.

Alliance Avenue, Ardoyne, Belfast

The stolen Audi screeched to a halt outside the café on the junction of Etna Drive. The passenger windows on the left side of the vehicle were already open.

Inside the café women and children watched out of the large window to witness the commotion outside.

The front seat passenger and his mate behind were wearing black ski masks and pointing pistols at the premises.

The women pushed their children beneath the tables as the first shots shattered the plate glass window sending shards of glass everywhere.

Bullets ricocheted off the walls, zipping like angry hornets above the terrified customers' heads.

The other rear seat passenger jumped from the car and threw a lighted milk bottle towards the now empty space. He was back in the vehicle as it wheel-spun away from the scene before the Molotov cocktail exploded just short of its intended target.

The heat singed one observer, but apart from a few glass cuts the injuries were minor.

Next day's newspapers began to speculate that dissident factions on both sides of the divide were about to return to an all-out conflict. Police resources were being drafted into the city and Bobby Charlton sat back and rubbed his hands in joy before cracking his fingers.

Rathcoole Estate, Antrim

Rathcoole, the Fort of Coole, was a large sprawling housing estate in Newtownabbey. A town famous for international footballers and a place where Republican icon Bobby Sands lived for a short time, before being 'relocated' by the local militia.

In the early '70s many Catholic residents of the town were forced out of the district and settled in Twinbrook in South Belfast, replaced by Protestants displaced from Republican estates in West Belfast.

The estate had been the scene of several sectarian murders and other violent crimes during the conflict. At around that time many disaffected young men became associated with the loyalist Tartan Gang in the domain named The Rathcoole KAI, the initials reportedly standing for Kill All Irish.

It was a terrific breeding ground for disaffected young unemployed Loyalists looking to vent their growing anger at the perceived Nationalist threat.

Dove slumped down into the armchair. He looked dog tired, his eyes were bloodshot red. The effects of the coke he had taken to keep him buzzing through the negotiations were beginning to wear off.

"You nearly got my head back in a fucking box, Bobby. Those fuckin' Micks down South are trying to become a Mexican cartel. I swear they're butchering kids down in Drogheda and Dublin." His Brummie accent was slurred due to the drugs.

"We need this next big shipment, Dovey. If we can just get rid of the Chinese fags on the Micks and then ship out the gear, they give us over to the boys in the West and the Scotland crews." The man limped over to the drinks cabinet and poured his Lieutenant another large whiskey into a heavy glass.

He was pleased that his plan was going well. With half the police force trying to keep the communities ripping each other apart his sordid deals with the drugs baron's shipments from the South could go on unmolested.

"We're playing with fire, Bobby. The new breed down South are mad men. One minute all calm and willing to play ball, then the next threatening to put your head in a vice and cut your balls off. I've dumped the gear they gave me at the farm for distribution. My boys will sort it out in the morning." His shoulders shrugged. They ached. He was ageing before his own eyes. The pressure was mounting daily.

The older man stood behind him and rested his hands on Dove.

"I've been asked about that other wee job!"

Dove sighed.

"Look, tell him it's ongoing. I met him at a bar in Manchester, but he was suspicious. He battered the Twins quite easily when they tried to snatch him. He's no ordinary soldier. When he left our unit, he just disappeared off the face of the earth. Special Forces for sure, I mean the information you gave me confirms that, so we need to be really careful. Guys like Phil Johnston could cause us significant damage."

"You're a sniper and now our best hit man, so sort the fucker out, before he gets more dangerous. I have a very interested party who wants him dead."

River Rooms, Donegall Quay, Belfast

The meal in the River Rooms on Donegall Quay was exquisite. Situated on the banks of the river Lagen, the building was the former home of sail and tent makers but had been transformed into a premier venue. Flusky was suitably impressed.

Her short armless sheer dress displayed her athletic arms and slim body. The lightness of her dress also gave an intriguing indentation of her pierced nipples. The hemline of the garment had ridden up showing the rose tattoo surrounded by barbed wire on her right thigh.

Other men sitting with their partners took sly glances in the direction of their table.

After finishing their meal, they walked down the three floors to the Cloud 9 cocktail bar in the basement. The great and good of Belfast were beginning to fill the room.

"So, you think your friend was involved in something, Phil?"

"No way. Winker was a good guy, straight as a die. I could trust him with my life. No, he's probably got involved with something he didn't even know. Poor fucker."

Corporal Watson was conscientious: he even reported himself when he was overpaid on expenses claim after a course. No, he certainly wasn't knowingly involved with paramilitaries; he trusted people on their word and might not have known if he was involved in a bigger plot.

Winker's main fault was giving people the benefit of the doubt. He always trusted his men to the hilt, people like Fusilier Dave Dove.

Parker's Ground Works, Co Antrim

Thomas Parker sat behind the desk in the cold portacabin. On the other side stood three men: two large, one small. All looked menacing.

A filing cabinet lay sideways on the office floor after being pushed over, with papers discarded from the open drawers littering the grubby carpet.

It was dark outside and the only illumination inside the office was a table light which shone in Parker's face.

A bruise was forming under his left eye; his hi-vis vest was torn and crumpled with several muddy boot prints on the back where they had stamped on his body.

"Apply for the contract and you'll get it. That's the deal."

"But Mister, that kinda job is way bigger than me or my boys can do. We do small clearances, not big blocks of flats. You need to speak to the Marshalls or Pomfrets, big boys. You're talking about four huge buildings. I wouldn't even be able to hold the quantity of explosive I need on my licence."

The small man in front reached inside his jacket and pulled out a 9mm Hi Power Browning pistol and laid it on the table. He had an English accent with just a hint of Irish which he had picked up over the years.

"I'm a bit of a clairvoyant, a bit of a gift, my old Mom used to say. It's my Romany roots, you know, Parker." He sat down opposite the sweating owner of the small demolitions company.

Parkers was a family business, employing men in the nearby community, supporting local charities. They even had their company logo on the shirts of a local football team. The owner, Thomas, was now trying to negotiate for his life.

The man reached back into his jacket and pulled out a long cylindrical black object and proceeded to screw it on to the barrel of the Browning.

"I see pain, never-ending pain, for the rest of your fookin' life, Mr Parker. If I don't shoot you the boys here will drill your knees."

One of the tall bald men standing behind the aggressor opened a green canvas bag and took out an ancient hand drill. The thug had tattoos up his neck and was smiling like a mad man.

"Apply, you will get the contract, it's a done deal. Don't worry about the manpower and other stuff, we'll sort that out on your behalf."

Parker was beaten. He looked down at his desk and nodded in agreement.

Gin Pit Woods

Granddad was taking his morning stroll with his dog, Fury, a brindle Staffordshire bull terrier. He often told his grandson that the dog was a mirror image of himself. He either wanted to fight or fuck.

The faithful dog stayed by his master's side, waiting to be unleashed. It looked around, scanning the path ahead and the dense undergrowth either side of the dirt track.

The old man became aware of his sixth sense, a tingling, an *absence of the normal, presence of the abnormal.*

Even the dog was more skittish than usual. It was a feeling he had learned to pay heed to. It had saved him on many occasions in Ireland.

He spotted the man standing by the anti-bike bollards which led deeper into the country park. He was standing aimlessly, appearing to wait for a friend. He was dressed in black; a hood covered his head, obscuring his face.

The plan had been to walk into Tyldesley for a morning coffee on the Square. Some of the older ladies would congregate after their early Zumba class. The dog was a good talking point with the females.

The dog started giving the tell-tale signs that he wanted to go and deposit last night's food, He looked up at Granddad and made a small whimpering noise, which was immediately obeyed.

The heavy brass clip attached to the strong leather leash was released and the small stocky terrier flew off along the track looking for solitude. The dog eyed the hooded man up ahead suspiciously.

The old man gave his dog some space then stepped off the track to pick up the stinking mess.

"I'm feeding you too much lad," he shouted after the jumping hound.

He bent and placed the waste in a black plastic doggy bag but didn't wrap the end. The smell was nauseous.

Granddad whistled as it sniffed in the low-lying bracken. "Suchup Fury!" he alerted the dog, who immediately changed posture to become alert to its wider surroundings, slowly turning to face the man blocking the way.

He resumed his walk towards the man, noticing that his well-trained dog had come to heel, never taking its eyes off the man dressed in black.

"Can I help you, mate?" the old man asked.

"Where's Johnno? Don't fuck me about, old man, or I'll slice you up." He removed a curved bladed dagger from the pouch pocket of his hoody.

"I hope you've got your balls in a tin box because Fury here is going to be chewing on them in a minute. Now fuck off and mug some other idiot before you get hurt."

"I need to speak to your grandson, Johnno, right now. Give me his fucking number or I'll find him at your funeral." The man took a step forward and walked into a face full of bull terrier shit launched underhand.

Blindly he lunged at Granddad, managing to slice through the sleeve of his jacket. Fury leapt to the defence of his master, locking on to the knee of the attacker.

Pops whiplashed the assailant with the thick leather dog lead, the heavy brass fastener hitting him in the forehead, opening up a small cut.

The man lashed out at the dog, making it yelp, releasing its grip. Unsteady, he held on to the bollards, retching with the smell, half blind and panicking. He half ran, half limped, barging into the old man as he escaped and knocking him down heavily on to the track.

Pops heard a loud crack as he hit the deck but forced himself to bounce back up on to his feet, fearing further attack.

He watched the man sprint off through the woods.

"No, Fury, stay!" he ordered his bleeding dog.

It had received a deep laceration on the back of its thick neck. The dog grumbled and dragged itself back to its master. It sat by its master's side, panting heavily, but still putting on a huge Staffy smile.

Burnside Park, Crawfordsburn

The morning train was stationary at a stop in Sydenham when Blue Eyes called him.

"Ma'am, how can I help?" he said, trying not to yawn.

"Good morning, Buster. We have had a further development, another murder this time in the city centre. The victim is a guy called Patrick Scott, a vagrant, but former soldier with your regiment."

Johnno looked out at the Unionist flags hanging limp which lined the streets.

"Two Platoon, just after I left. He was at the reunion the other night as well, drunk as a lord."

"Well, it's taken a while to find his body, he was violently assaulted, then thrown in the canal. We think his body was caught under a ledge for a while until a passing narrowboat's wash brought it to the surface. First response was that he was a drunk that drowned then hit by a boat, but the coroner found some slash marks."

GMP had struggled with the identification: it took days for the fingerprints to be finally identified as those of the former soldier.

Johnno thought about the latest murder.

"Scott was the Platoon Sergeant on a deployment to Belfast. One of his troop's called Rattigan was abducted during a riot and was rescued from an IRA safehouse," he explained.

Were the attacks a result of Rattigan's kidnap? He was sure that the two guys that tried to attack him in Manchester were from the orange side of the fence. If they had been sent by the Republicans, he probably would be dead.

Rattigan had the main motive to kill his former Platoon Sergeant, but why the other troops?

"Thanks for letting me know." he said before hitting the red off button.

He put the thought to the back of his mind and thought about what he was going to say to his former lover.

He stifled another yawn; he could still smell Flusky's perfume in his nostrils from the night before. They had both woken early and gone running through the deserted city with just the council street cleaners for company.

After the run they had made love again in the small shower, intense, passionate. He was an avid reader of Lee Child's books in which the main protagonist, Jack Reacher, always claimed that the second one was always the best. So far, his trip to Belfast had certainly confirmed that theory.

He exited the train at Helen's Bay and took a quick taxi ride to Crawfordsburn, a small overspill village outside Bangor. The cab dropped him on the far side of the estate, and he walked away from his intended destination after paying the fare.

In Ireland it was best practice never to tell cabbies your business or let them drop you off outside the exact premises.

It took him ten minutes to walk around the roads to ensure he wasn't being followed. Once he was happy, he entered Burnside Park.

Donna and her family lived in a white-walled extended bungalow surrounded by a well-tended lawn.

It matched exactly the description given to him by Tom.

A young man answered the ring of the bell, he was stocky, dark hair, dark eyes, tanned, fit, and smiling. Winker was tall, wiry, blue eyes, ginger and didn't know how to smile.

"Uncle Phil?" he enquired. "Mommies in the kitchen. Take yourself in." He pointed in a vague direction and shouted 'goodbye' over his shoulder as he began his journey to college. The last time Johnno had seen him was when he was a toddler.

She appeared in the hallway with a large steaming mug.

Donna Watson had hardly changed since he had last seen her, apart from her hair style, which had changed from a bobbed blonde to short and choppy with purple tones. She was small, elfin-like, pale skin, cute freckles beneath her grey-blue eyes with long natural lashes.

A mother of three and always on the go, cleaning her home or working at the local pharmacy. She nervously puffed on a vape, emitting a smell of oily strawberries into the air.

She pointed the way to the spacious living room. It looked like it was ready for an inspection.

They sat opposite each other. She still hadn't looked him directly in the eyes, head bowed as if trying to deal with a guilty secret.

"Donna, your son is he..."

She had tears already welling up. She took another puff, trying to gather the right words for her confession.

"He's our son, not Winker's. I wanted to tell you and I should have told you, but would it have made any difference? You had your family and your job which you were obsessive about."

He felt like he had been stabbed in the heart.

"He's about the same age as my son, Jamie. Looks like him too," he observed.

"Peter has just started at the college. He wants to be a policeman, or a soldier would you believe. It must be in his genes."

There was a strained silence.

"Look, Donna, I didn't have a clue, but I'll do my best to help you and Peter. Just say what you want."

Her eyes narrowed.

"Why the hell do I want anything from you? You gave me a beautiful son for which I'm grateful. We had some good times, it was an adventure, and Winker wasn't the most vigorous man between the sheets, but that part of my life is over."

He held up his hands in mock surrender.

"OK, but I do need to talk about Winker and the months before he disappeared."

She sipped on her tea to clear her throat and compose herself.

Winker, with Johnno's help, had reached the rank of Sergeant Major. He was flying through the ranks with people in high places commenting that he was destined to become the RSM and possibly a commissioned officer. That all stopped when his hips started giving him trouble.

He was moved sideways to the Motor Transport Platoon. Not happy with his future career options he chose to terminate his service, taking a decent pension to re-join civilian life.

He had spent his time with the MT Platoon well, doing all the courses he could to help his move back to civvy street. He was a driving and HAZMAT instructor so when he left the military, he rapidly got employment with an oil distribution company, occasionally doing some driving to keep his hand in.

On one such journey he was stopped in South Armagh and was challenged about the tattoo on his right arm: red and white hackle OAFAAF. Although the men didn't know that it stood for Once A Fusilier Always A Fusilier, they did recognise that it had a British military connotation.

He regained consciousness beside his blazing truck: the oil trailer had been stolen. They had beaten him badly and left him for dead.

He took an age to recover, and quickly left the job with depression and PTSD.

"He started working for a company over in Ballyclare, Fast Move, delivery driving. He had bumped into another ex-Fusilier he called Dovey when we were out shopping in Bangor. They had him driving over to the mainland or picking up boxes from Dublin. It was a crap job, but the money was great. Then Tom suggested going to the reunion and he never came back." She started to cry.

He moved to sit beside her on the white sofa. He held her hand and kissed her forehead.

She reached for the back of his head, looking into his eyes. The same old feelings she had been trying to repress came flooding back.

They kissed.

His phone began to vibrate: Sharon. He chose to ignore the call and placed his hands behind Donna's head and drew her lips towards him. His phone pinged.

He sighed and looked at the message.

'Pops attacked, in Wigan A&E. Come home immediately.'

CHAPTER SIX

A&E, King Edward Royal Infirmary, Wigan

Phil had rung Sharon from the airport as he was about to board the plane back to Manchester. He had been in such a panic that he had left Donna's front door wide open as he sprinted out of her house and ran to the train station.

When he walked on to the ward Pops was sitting up in bed smiling. A nurse from Senegal was checking his blood pressure and making small talk.

"Roukia, this is my grandson, Phil," he mumbled whilst juggling with the thermometer between his lips.

She turned and gave him a beaming smile.

"Pleased to meet you, Mister Phil," she breathed.

"Your Grandfather is on the mend, he's a very brave man and very naughty," she giggled as she noted all the readings on a clipboard.

The patient had a large purple bruise under his right eye and there was thick wrapping on his right upper arm. He had a bridge built into his bed covers preventing any undue weight onto the repairs to his broken hip.

"Struth, Pops, that's some hard on!" he joked, pointing at the bridge."

"Don't make me laugh," the old mad said in obvious discomfort.

"I think you'll be on the bench this weekend, Pops."

The old man laughed again and pointed to a vacant chair.

"That fucker was looking for you, asked where Johnno was."

"Was he Irish?" Johnno asked.

"No, local lad – tall, skinny, pale hands, and a face full of dog shit. I told the police it probably was a jealous husband. I hit the attacker in the eye with the lead and Fury bit him on the leg. They've taken the dog's lead to check for DNA."

"Well, your coat is a write off and Fury has twenty stitches in his back and collar. Sharon has him at her place. She's going mad trying to stop him shagging her cats."

The old man winced in pain as he laughed.

"Sharon tells me you were in Belfast, son."

Johnno nodded in agreement.

"I have a contact in Ireland that might be able to help. Her code name was Credlin, but her real name is Katie "Ma" Fitzpatrick. She was a leading Provo, commanding the Cumann na mBan women's section in Belfast before moving over to Sinn Fein. She owes me."

"Wrong side of the wall, Pops. These guys are more than likely Prods. She won't be able to help. I'm sorry you've been mixed up in this," he sighed.

The old man reached out and grabbed his grandson's hand. He squeezed it tightly to get his full attention.

"Listen and learn, the Republicans know more about the Loyalists than any cop or spook. They have always been one step ahead of the opposition. We had to help the Orange side to keep it a fair playing field. Go and see Ma, she'll help you, I promise."

Monkscoole House, Rathcoole

A plain white sheet covered the body with smaller sheets covering pieces splattered at a greater range after the fall from the balcony of one of the flats. Yellow numbered triangles marked each area as a potential source of evidence.

A small police cordon had been erected whilst the forensic officers conducted a fingertip search. A small crowd had gathered, some taking pictures on their mobile phones, others bringing bunches of flowers.

Four tall white accommodation blocks stood tall and white dominating the scene. The body had fallen from a great height judging by the amount of real estate his shattered body and blood was covering.

Two men watched from a window of the tenth floor of Abbotscoole House, both chuckled.

"That will teach that fuckin' grass from jumping without checking his parachute," one remarked. He rubbed his still bruised and swollen knee.

"Come on, finish your fag. The little Brummie bastard wants us to relocate the women to a new knocking shop. He's just relocated the family that lived there."

The other man spat out and flicked his cig butt over the balcony, not caring whom it hit on landing.

"That wee fucker nearly got us killed in Manchester, trying to snatch that fella, Bro. I swear the next time we have to grab him I'll shoot the fucker in the leg first."

"He wants us to go back over to Manchester, he says he has an address he wants us to check out and maybe put some pressure on the guy, so you might get your chance to kneecap the wee fucker."

Cadishead Way, Irlam Wharf Road

It hadn't taken long to find Rattigan, He was leaving a chemist with a large brown bag of prescription drugs and wearing an eye patch which wasn't big enough to cover the dark purple bruising.

MIT were probably still awaiting the results of the blood coming back from the dog lead before they identified him as the perpetrator of the attack.

Johnno had no doubts at all who the perpetrator of the attack was.

DCI Wood hadn't given him any further mention during her last update.

He had rung Little P and asked if any new jobs had landed from their recent tasking, so he could start planning his work schedule after he returned from leave.

Nothing new, drugs dealers in South Manchester and armed blaggers in Salford were the flavours of the month.

Johnno had waited for him to return to his flat before making an approach. As he locked the car door he spotted Rattigan on the move again, getting in to a VW Beetle and driving off from the small estate.

He weaved his way out of Eccles and through the Old Trafford industrial estate before going under the M60 Manchester orbital road. His beat-up car then entered the Cadishead Way and Irlam Wharf Road Universal Container Terminal.

Johnno could have followed Rattigan in an ice cream van with the jingles playing full blast and still not be compromised. His target was in the doldrums. Head down, switched off. His security was lax.

Bright halogen lights illuminated the entrance and a gate guard stepped out of a portacabin to check the driver.

The surveillance officer drove past the entrance, checking the CCTV and dome camera arrangements which followed the line of wire fencing and galvanised steel with razor wire on top.

At the end of the fence was grass land and a hill to the west. A path used by dog walkers led from a small parking spot between the trees towards the cold waters of the ship canal.

He parked his car by the entrance to the small, wooded area at the south of the freighter terminal and entered the trees.

Although the security coverage along Cadishead Way was good the same could not be said for the southern boundary. A simple steel fence which was not properly deeply embedded would probably stop an elderly dog walker but not a seasoned professional watcher.

It took a short while for his eyes to adjust to the bright lights of the compound. He noted that all the surveillance cameras covered outwards and not in towards the yard which was divided into sections by large oblong ISO containers of different sizes and colours.

Occasionally a huge forklift vehicle or small crane would appear and lift one of the boxes and whisk it away towards a waiting truck.

Several times he moved position to get a better view of the yard. It was after midnight then he spotted him.

Rattigan was wearing a thick luminous jacket with SECURITY written on the back. A white safety helmet and glasses bobbled on his scrawny head.

He held a clipboard and moved to a column of orange containers. Phil started creeping forward to position himself behind the guard.

A breeze was coming from the direction of the ship canal. Two ships were at anchor: a large green and white container ship and a red and black bulk container that was being unloaded by a huge bucket crane. An orange dust was catching in the light breeze and being distributed over a wide area of the jetty.

Ratty pulled open the door of a long orange Hapag-Lloyd ISO container and peered into the darkness. The container was empty and echoed.

He pulled at the wood lining of the container; a container of cigarettes fell to the floor.

The size eight boot hit Ratty in the centre of his back and propelled him face-first on to the floor of the box. He heard the creaking of the hinges as the door was slammed shut and the levers locking the door pushed into position, trapping him in the darkness.

He began to convulse in the pitch black. Darkness was one of his many fears.

He was immediately dragged back to the black bag on his head in Belfast, the unseen punches, and assaults. The unseen persons screaming abuse in his ears.

"Let me out," he screamed.

He felt his way back towards the door and kicked out at the metal.

"Calm down Ratty, I just want to ask you some questions."

The razor-sharp pointed blade of a curved knife suddenly appeared and started cutting at the rubber dampening which surrounded the doors.

"Let me out, I'll fucking kill you!" The screaming was manic, from a deranged trapped beast.

"Calm down, buddy. Who are you working for? Tell me and I'll open the door," he promised.

The doors of the ISO container boomed loudly as Rattigan tried to barge his way to freedom.

"Dovey, I work for Dovey, he wants me to find you for a friend," he sobbed.

"Why?"

"His friend is very rich and will pay for me to visit the best cancer specialists in America. Now let me go." He was quickly becoming hoarse with the screaming.

"Why me, Ratty, why does Dove want me?" he asked calmly, trying to pacify his prisoner.

"Ireland, something about Ireland," he sobbed.

There was silence. Johnno shouted louder and banged on the door to try and get a reaction.

Johnno dialled Blue Eyes. Within twenty minutes she stood beside him as armed response officers shouted a warning and opened the door of the ISO container.

The flashlights underneath their machine guns picked out the prone figure laid flat on the floor.

Blood splatters decorated the roof and walls. He had severed his throat arteries and bled out in less than two minutes. Ratty's forehead was a mess where he had tried to ram his way out of his tomb with his head.

"Clear!" the officers shouted in unison.

"I warned you about getting involved. You should have called me earlier." She scowled at him.

"How the fuck was I supposed to know he was psychotic? He attacked my Granddad. Have you considered just how he got his details? There must be a grass in GMP. Someone has checked my P file. Granddad's details are on it. Oh fuck!"

"What?"

"Sharon and the kids' address is also on that file."

Shackley Road, Tyldesley

He answered the door wearing just shorts and a t-shirt. He was cooking pasta and wasn't expecting any visitors, so he had made sure he checked through the upstairs window before answering.

He had checked on Sharon and their children. All were safe, but he reiterated the warning that they needed to remain vigilant. For once his ex-wife agreed with him.

He had seen the blonde hair and breathed a huge sigh of relief. She was carrying a large white day book with further pieces of paper stuffed between its pages.

"Good evening, Boss. Home visits now?"

"Well, my dinner is in the dog, so I thought I'd better speak to you in person instead of phoning."

She looked tired and a little dishevelled. Her blonde hair was uncombed.

"Your partner a good cook? I have something on which I can share if you're hungry."

"That'd be great, and yes, she's a really good cook."

He showed her through to a small lounge and poured her a glass of red wine.

The room was very tidy but in definite need of a woman's touch. No bric-a-brac or photographs were on display. A simple square mirror was the only feature on the wall.

The latest model TV sat above the latest model DVD player and sound bar which was probably the latest model. A bank of DVD boxes was arranged in neat lines. The word regimental sprung to mind.

There were no hanging police commendations of which she knew he had many, or memorabilia of his military career or family pictures. Anybody entering the house would have no clues as to who owned the property - apart from that they were tech geeks.

Over dinner she told him that they had recovered a mat black karambit knife which was possibly the murder weapon used on the victims which her team were investigating. They had also found a smashed-up burner phone which had been pieced together and had been calling another phone in Northern Ireland.

Blood from Fury's leash was a match for the now deceased Mr Rattigan.

The forensic team had also been suspicious about the cigarette packages and the inner dimensions of the ISO container.

When they removed one of the hardwood panelling boards, they found thousands of boxes of Chinese cigarettes. The Chinese counterfeits emitted higher levels of dangerous chemicals than brand-name cigarettes: eighty percent more nicotine and a staggering one hundred and thirty percent more carbon monoxide, and they contained impurities that included insect eggs and human faeces.

The container had entered the port legitimately, carrying machine parts. Her detectives were now looking at the theory that Rattigan was the man who would allow the box to be picked up by an unlicensed truck and spirited away.

"You might get a result by looking at the accident that occurred to his mate, Eddie Walpole, who was crushed on top of one of those ISO containers. Perhaps he saw something that Rattigan didn't want him to see and murdered him as well."

She picked up her day book and noted down yet another action for her officers.

She had quickly got a warrant together and detectives were conducting a detailed search of Rattigan's flat and car.

"He said he was doing this to get treatment for cancer."

She put her empty plate down on a coffee table.

"Yes, we have checked his medical records and found nothing. He had a bit of IBS but no cancers. He was a constant visitor to his local surgery, and A&E. Someone commentated that he should have been invited to the Hospital Christmas party. He was an NHS nightmare."

Johnno thought that Ratty's hypochondria might have been triggered by the PTSD he suffered with.

"I heard you've been suspended. Sorry about that, but I'm sure you'll be re-instated once we conclude or investigations," she spoke.

"You don't get it, do you? Rattigan's death won't stop this. The people you're dealing with will stop at nothing to kill me or my family."

"Why does the IRA want you dead?"

He groaned. "It's not the IRA or any other Republican group. This threat is coming from the Loyalists."

"But aren't they friends with us? And why attack a former British soldier. What have you done?"

"That's why I need to return to Belfast and why you need to find out who looked at my file."

CHAPTER SEVEN

Premier Inn, Cathedral District, Belfast

Gordon Henderson stood outside the hotel waiting for his former colleague. Hendo was a former technical guru with the Royal Signals before passing selection to join the highly secretive Special Forces Signals Squadron as a covert operator.

For years Hendo had been installing covert observation and listening devices, some of which he had designed himself.

He was now a civilian working for MI5 and still inventing and deploying covert devices, but his new speciality was mobile phones. He was the best in the business at tracking and bugging the very latest devices on the market.

He had been told that his former team leader had flown into the Province that morning and been picked up by a beautiful woman at the International airport in Aldergrove before being dropped off at the hotel.

Johnno almost knocked him off his feet as he launched himself out of the door, looking down at an address written down by his Granddad on a small piece of paper.

"Fuck me, Phillip, mind your step!" Hendo sounded like an officer and dressed like one as well. It always led the troops in the Squadron to take the piss.

He pointed over towards Blinkers Restaurant so Johnno, intrigued, followed.

Hendo ordered an all-day fry. A plate of heart attack. He was still stick thin but could eat a horse without putting on an ounce. He claimed he was working with PSNI, he didn't say which department. His hair was longer, greyer and his eyes sunk deeper into his skull.

It was Hendo told anybody that would listen that it was his great phone work and cross referencing with the available CCTV that had led Johnno's team to the address which had rescued young Fusilier

Rattigan. The Operation Masquerade release was the pinnacle of his career.

Hendo always failed to mention the importance of the informer that had passed on the phone number of the Republican dissident that was holding the young soldier.

Johnno lent back in his chair and chewed his dry toast and sipped his tea whilst Hendo quickly devoured the huge breakfast.

"Hungry?" he commented.

"Food is fuel, never to be enjoyed." He burped, whilst wiping bean juice off his chin.

"Phos wants to talk to you. I'm here to give you a lift to Palace," he said as he rose to his feet, not waiting for Johnno to finish his food.

Loughside, MI5 HQ, Belfast

Hendo had given Phil exactly ten minutes to shower and change before whisking him at high speed out of the city.

The red brick barrack blocks of Palace Barracks sat on the site known as "Ardtullagh", the home of the Bishop of Down, Connor and Dromore. As well as soldiers the camp had recently received new residents in the shape of MI5.

The new MI5 HQ Lough View was located in the centre of the military compound. It had been built on the site of Johnno's grandad's old unit the MRF. The high grey wriggly tin walls were long gone replaced by a green security fence, memorial garden, and trees.

Brigadier John 'Phos' Mathews, former Commanding Officer Special Surveillance Unit, was now a big cheese in Whitehall. He had re-cap badged from his Infantry regiment to the Intelligence Corps and then jumped up the ranks even further after secondments to the nation's security departments.

Phos was a good man, a leader from the front which was evidenced by his award of a Military Cross. His men loved him.

Not afraid to chew someone's arse but then protect them like a tigress protecting her precious cubs. He was given the nickname Phos after the smoke screen instantaneously produced from a phosphorus grenade.

He was good at screening his troops from the eyes of the upper echelons of command until they had sorted out any bumps in the road.

He was sociable, his door always open and in the midst of all the pranks when the guys let their hair down.

Now Phos was the Senior Military Liaison Officer for MI5. His office was completely sanitised. No papers, only a computer and Security Service mouse mat. He spent his days running between his Lough View office and Stormont, the seat of the Northern Ireland Assembly.

The office was minimalist: a glass table, black leather relining work chair. Two Chesterfield ox blood chairs sat either side of a large ox blood sofa. The clear glass walls gave a view out on to the blue carpeted open plan office.

A green stencilled picture of Churchill was on the far wall. Below the face was the quote, 'Never give in. *'Never, never, never, never-- in nothing, great or small, large or petty--never give in.'*'

"I like what you've done with the place, Boss," Johnno quipped.

They hugged whilst Hendo disappeared to get the kettle on.

"I know why you're here. I'm surprised you haven't asked for help."

"I'm not sure I need any help yet, John, I have a rough idea that these murders of my old platoon are trying to flush me out into the open for something in my past."

"And what transgressions do you think you've made?" John asked.

He pushed back into the leather, making it creak.

"Where do I start? Jealous husband probably. All the operations I worked on with the Det are subject to the seventy-year rule. No books have mentioned what we got up to and even the historical crime team have left me and the team alone."

"Recompense," his former boss whispered.

"Recompense?"

He thought hard about the word, then it all came flooding back to him.

"The job down in West Belfast - we did it for the source handling unit. That was all done and dusted. Complete exoneration. PSNI, lawyers, even the families had no comebacks. Plus, the reporting restrictions on the job were draconian, because of the agents we had in play."

"We think that somebody has been talking about the job, one of our own. We had a guy that tried to re-connect to his former handlers. Smug, by all accounts. His opening comment was that he knew all about Recompense and the people that were also interested in the murders."

"Murders, what murders? The guy who fired at us was shot, driver died of his injuries, passenger was an own goal by his fleeing mate who subsequently escaped as per the plan."

"A friend of the informer that escaped that night was a cellmate on the mainland with Alan Sampey."

Corporal Alan Sampey was the driver of the Mercedes G wagon on the night of the ambush. Recompense was his last operation. After the incident he began to get severe migraine, vivid flashbacks. The bullet which ripped out the throat of the passenger had also followed through and hit him in the chest. Luckily his body armour had stopped any major damage.

He had returned to his unit in Germany shortly afterwards and proceeded to drink himself to an unsavoury discharge. Drink turned to drugs which led to prison in both Germany and back at home in England.

Rumours started spreading through the prison service that he was becoming a radicalised Christian.

Delusions about Cromwell's actions in Ireland and the need to eradicate any Finian. He was a devout listener of evangelical pastors and conspiracy theorists.

Lashing out at prisoners of any other religion. He became of interest to the Counter Terrorism Prison Intelligence Unit who debriefed him.

He disclosed a list of 'murders' carried out by the British forces of occupation against the Protestant community during the Troubles. He was both a danger to himself and the state.

"Sampey went rogue on us and before he was moved to a more secure unit, he had been a cellmate with a few prisoners we would not have liked him talking to. One of which was our little blabbermouth now talking about Recompense."

Johnno thought long and hard about the new information. Betrayal was part and parcel of operations in Northern Ireland if you were a terrorist, but now the boot was on the other foot.

"So, who is the new informant, and when are you going to bump him next?"

"Curbishley, he's called, and he said he was a friend of the UVF Commander in Rathcoole, a guy called Charlton."

"Charlton was the tout who escaped, wasn't he?"

"The very same man, and he's still on the books. He gives us bits and pieces from time to time, but he's a man on the move with his name on many charitable organisations, councils, and he's even an advisor on the police board." He passed Johnno a piece of paper.

"Look, here's an email address. I want you to visit your old chum Sampey in Long Lartin. The Security unit has your details and will organise a legal visit. They think you're going to debrief him about the Official Secrets Act. The head shed here are keeping it tight. In the meantime, I'll get Charlton's handlers to give him a nudge."

The thought of his former colleague Sampey being in prison then colluding with their former enemies made his blood boil.

"There's another guy called Dove that's over here. He was at a recent reunion. I was told that he has links to the paramilitaries. I got the impression that he wanted more than a social chat with me."

Phos rubbed his chin.

"Dove works for Charlton, but surprisingly Charlton hardly mentions him as if he's trying to protect him. Lots of rumours and finger pointing about how an ex-soldier can live in South East Antrim without being involved. PSNI are convinced that Dove carries a 9mm Browning Hi Power he stole from the armoury in Ballykinler. Been used in murders and punishment shootings - Gun Twenty-Two the cops call it due to the number of times it's been forensically linked to ongoing police investigations."

Charlton was a real chancer; he had taken over a huge market from Loyalist dealers involved in drugs importation from China. Now the Chinese market was drying up supplying drugs he was looking for new suppliers.

China was still supplying huge amounts of illegal cigarettes and counterfeit goods including prescription drugs, but cocaine, ecstasy and cannabis in large quantities was the commodities they required.

"What about Curbishley?" Johnno asked.

"Literally a dead end because somebody launched him out of a tower block a few days ago. It looks like somebody is doing a little housekeeping."

Beechfield Street, Short Strand

There were the sounds of kids playing noisily in the playground of the McArthur Nursery School. He could hear the kids but could not see them.

The school was on the other side of a peace wall, a red brick divider over ten feet high with a larger metal fence on top to stop missiles being thrown over from the Loyalist or Nationalist community.

She lived on the front line, her home covered by CCTV cameras.

He knocked on the front door and stepped back down off the front step. She had been expecting his call and was happy to arrange his visit. Pops must have still been in touch with his old agent. Strictly against the rules, but then again rules had never stood in the old man's way in the past.

A middle-aged man opened the door. He looked at the new arrival with suspicion.

"I'm Phil, I have an appointment to see Mrs Fitzpatrick," he explained.

The man pointed inside and followed Johnno into a second, secure holding room. He closed the door behind them and operated an electric switch which double bolted the front entrance. He noticed it shut with a clunk, possibly it was lead lined.

After a rough search a second inner door was released, and he was allowed access into the house.

She was waiting to greet him but stayed back until her bodyguard had disappeared before she spoke.

"So, young man, let me look at you." She raised her glasses to the bridge of her nose and walked around him.

"I wonder if that little arse of yours is as fast as your Granddad's," she teased.

"What did that old bastard call me - Kate Fitzpatrick. 'Machine Gun Kate' or Agent Credlin?"

"He called you Ma."

She smiled and led him into an airy kitchen. There was a smell of recent paint and freshly baked bread.

Over a cup of tea, they discussed the past and present. She had a twinkle in her eye every time she mentioned 'That old bugger.'

His Granddad had recruited her when she was at a crossroads in her thinking, swaying from armed conflict to political settlement. The Ballot Box, not the ArmaLite.

"I called him 'Bucky' because he would buck anything in a skirt," she admitted.

"Including you, Ma?" he teased.

She looked flushed and sheepish. Her hair dyed raven black, she was a big buxom woman, her large cleavage on display. She would have been a stunner back in her day and he didn't doubt for one moment that his old Granddad hadn't at least tried to make a pass at his agent.

Ma had been involved in a number of skirmishes with both the police and the army. Some male members of her organisation had started becoming jealous of this jumped-up woman's success and began to start making remarks about her ability to pull off spectacular successes against the security forces.

His Granddad had stepped in, recruited her, even whisked her away to safety when she was about to be arrested and interrogated by the Provos' infamous 'Nutting Squad', a group of assassins who provided internal security for the Republican movement.

Granddad had managed to rid her of the men of violence who stood in her way. He placed her on a different path, introduced her to people who would nourish her enthusiasm, politicise her. He was a visionary, and she loved him for it.

The house had been extended to a high standard; it was well decorated. A few children's toys were on display - great grandchildren, she explained. She looked at him again.

"So, what did you do over here, Phillip?" she asked, her accent soft and warm.

"I was just a soldier, a thinking soldier doing my job, Ma."

She smiled. "No ordinary soldier, you, my boy. You have the look and ways of Bucky. What were you?"

There was a silence. He felt like a distance was growing between them, something which he wanted to avoid. He might need her knowledge in the near future.

"Just a volunteer, the same as you and your comrades. Doing my duty as best I could."

The smile returned to her face.

"I can help you, just sit here a while." She patted his knee and walked towards the front room.

He could hear her talking to a man, probably the guy who had shown him in.

She returned and handed him a small black PDA. The Personal Digital Assistant was no bigger than his mobile phone. He looked up at Ma in puzzlement.

"What?" she asked.

"Don't you think we've moved on from passing communications written on Rizla papers? This device is encrypted. If anyone tries to download the information which is stored on it the machine will drop everything."

He rolled it over in his hand, impressed.

"So, what's on it?"

"The complete details of the Loyalist movement. Take it and use it with our blessings."

"How do you know I'm interested in Loyalists?"

"Because if you were looking for Republicans we would know, and you would probably be dead already."

She hugged and kissed his cheek when he stood to leave, with a promise that she would update him on any developments.

"Be very careful, young man, and trust no one, not even the police. They're not on your side anymore," she reminded him.

He turned to walk away.

"Phillip, the Loyalists are trying to start the war again. Its none of our doing and we'll put a stop to it once we get the guilty party."

"Why are they doing that, Ma? Nobody wants the Troubles to return."

"Smoke and mirrors, son."

He got the feeling that she knew exactly who was behind the new wave of violence.

Premier Inn, Cathedral District, Belfast

In the quiet of his hotel room, he entered the password she had made him remember and the PDA came to life.

The Protestant paramilitaries were split into two groups. The UVF, Ulster Volunteer Force, was formed by an ex-British Soldier in 1965. They had been attacking Nationalist targets for over thirty years, including infamous attacks in Dublin and Monaghan.

They had a number of flags of convenience satellite organisations which took the wrap for some of their more heinous crimes.

Since the peace agreement had been signed, they had lost their way. PSNI's Paramilitary Crime Task Force had made major inroads in to the group's criminality seizing drugs, cash, expensive cars, and jewellery.

They didn't fare much better as guardians of their community as police estimated that over eighty per cent of their victims were innocent with no links at all to the Republican movement. Since the 1994 ceasefire the UVF had killed at least thirty-two people, twenty-nine of whom were Protestant.

The commanders called themselves Brigadiers and made a fortune from racketeering and the taxing of its own men. The organisation was hopelessly split between the Shankill Road leadership and the East Belfast faction.

He read a comment which stated that ninety per cent of its members expressed a desire to leave the terror gang during an internal debate but were refused.

'The whole organisation is a mess, almost everyone to a man wants it to pack up and go except for the ones at the top.'

He noted that the UVF were organised along the same lines as the British Army. The Provo spies had the full details of each unit and location of its recruitment area.

The 1st Battalion was situated on the Shankill Road and designated as the headquarters. The 1st Battalion was then split into four companies:

A Company on the Shankill Road

B Company in the Woodvale area.

C Company spread between the Glencairn and Springmartin estates.

D Company up in Ballysillan.

All in all, about a thousand men of which only twenty were operators or active daily, the others were just cannon fodder. The leadership had recruited a lot of drug dealers, press ganged into selling for the UVF or receiving a punishment beating or shooting.

Anybody who ran up a bar tab in one of the UVF-controlled drinking dens or were using one of the money-lending schemes were forced to pay off their debt by turning up at marches or committing an act of violence.

The 2nd Battalion was in South Belfast, the Village, and Donegal Pass, and the larger 3rd Battalion in North Belfast. Its companies were organised into detachments along the Shore Road and stretched into Tiger's Bay, Mount Vernon, and Rathcoole.

The 3rd Battalion Commander had grandiose ideas about his organisation and declared that he was the leader of the North Belfast & East Antrim Brigade, to the consternation of the other Brigadiers.

The other Loyalist organisation was the Ulster Defence Association (UDA) It was formed in 1971 as an umbrella group for various Loyalist groups. Their flag of convenience unit was the Ulster Freedom Fighters (UFF) who took the rap for a lot of their atrocities.

Johnno had remembered most of each group's history from his previous tours. He had been mainly engaged in operations in the Nationalist areas of North and West Belfast, but on occasions his team was called upon to support the police in counteracting Loyalist gangs.

There were detailed files on members of each group, including addresses and places of work. The intelligence dossier was better and more substantial than anything he had seen produced by the police or Intelligence Corps analysts.

The files were littered with covert pictures of front doors of home addresses of proposed targets, primary Loyalists figures and detailed timetables of school runs, sporting events and trips to drinking dens.

He continued to scroll through the details when he spotted a familiar name.

Robert "Bobby" Charlton sat on the Antrim and Newtownabbey policing board and quite a few other 'charitable' organisations. He was allegedly close to the local MP, Sir John Smythe. Charlton was the commander of North Belfast & East Antrim Brigade with grand ideas above his station.

There were pictures of Loyalist leaders shaking hands with other men. A caption underneath explained that the other men were high ranking policemen or former senior officers in the disbanded Ulster Defence Regiment.

He then opened up another file which was marked 'Of Interest' The first thing he saw was a covertly taken picture of a group of men standing laughing on a street corner. The picture was grainy, but Johnno recognised the small man in the centre of the frame: Dove, without question.

Dove was of great interest to the Republicans. A file indicated that he was wanted for anti-social behaviour. He had been supplying drug dealers on Nationalist estates. There was also a claim that he was a conduit between a cartel in Dublin, but it was the last line of the pen picture which made him shiver.

"Dove is believed to be the North Howard Street sniper."

Carson Street, Larne

Fat Tommy Taylor slowly trudged up the hill towards his home. He was carrying a white plastic bag, his twenty-five stone bulk wobbling as he placed one weary step in front of another, his bulbous belly hanging over his dirty dark grey fleece jogging bottoms.

His long greasy hair was unkempt. Johnno had tracked his movement down to the off licence Winemark on Broadway and back again.

Taylor wheezed as he climbed the five steps up to the door of his house, then entered.

The light was fading as Johnno walked further up the hill and turned left on to Rugby Terrace. A few lights were illuminating upstairs bedrooms in some of the terraced houses.

He walked a few paces and looked down the small alleyway that snaked off back down the hill to his left, giving access to the rear yards of the Carson Street homes.

Earlier in the day he had walked down the alley. He was carrying a dog lead. If anybody would have seen him, they would have thought it was just a guy looking for his stray pooch.

A grey metal famer's fence was part way down the alley which led into the back garden of Taylor's house.

A few empty flower pots and some dead plants were scattered around the concrete yard. A rusty old bike was propped up against an old shed with a broken window pane. The smell from the drains indicated that they needed unblocking.

He had identified the ageing back door as his entry point and had easily jemmied the latch with a Spyderco lock knife. There was a smell of stale sweat, dampness, and squalor as he cautiously entered, slowly closing the door behind him.

The small kitchen was in darkness. It was dirty, full of old take away cartons. Bins and work surfaces were overflowing. A steam iron looked out of place. Thick black patches which looked like burnt rubber.

He peeped inside the downstairs bathroom; it looked like the shower hadn't been used for a while. The toilet was dirty, using wet wipes and newspaper to wipe his fat arse. No wonder the drains were blocked.

Beyond the kitchen was a large living room. Curtains on the bay windows were closed, only a small amount of light emanating from a TV shone through. There were sounds of a child screaming from the large over 60-inch TV which filled the bay window space.

The smell of sweat and alcohol in the living room almost made him retch as he crept up upon the man sitting on the large suite facing the TV.

Johnno fought the urge to look at the TV screen, not sure if it was a computer feed, DVD, or pen drive. Taylor was engrossed with the action. His fat stubby fingers were buried in his pants.

Another scream from the TV made him involuntarily raise his head. A small naked boy was crying he was bound to a bed and being tortured by a man with a red-hot poker. He now realised what was on the iron in the kitchen.

Fat boy was aroused; beads of sweat ran down his jowls.

Johnno felt the anger rise in his body. He fought to control the rage, control it, channel it, but his revulsion at the image was overpowering.

He clenched his fist and smashed the sitting man behind the ear as hard as he could.

When Taylor woke, he was cold, naked, and hog-tied. Several pen drives and DVDs were neatly lined up on the dirty settee.

"Looks like you've been a naughty boy, Thomas. Playing out your fantasy for real, I think." There was a hiss as steam came from the warming iron. Droplets of evaporating steam fell on the restrained man's white arse cheeks which made them wobble uncontrollably.

The man began to sob Johnno held the iron above the still-wobbling flesh.

"Do the cops know you live so close to Larne Grammar School, Thomas? Surely there's some kind of exclusion order to keep a predator like you away from schoolboys."

The sobbing increased.

"Listen, you fat fucker, I don't care about your little indiscretions, but I do want to know about an Englishmen called Dove, and what happened to a guy he met on the ferry last year."

He lied: he was more than pissed about Taylor's behaviour, but he needed answers.

"I know you met Dove on a ferry crossing. Also on that boat was a good friend of mine, a tall ginger headed guy. A father of three children."

He placed the iron closer to Taylor's skin. He could see redness forming as it heated up the flesh.

Taylor began to howl and whimper.

"You're a big guy, Taylor, lots of flab to iron. This might take hours unless you talk. Burns, eh! Fuckin' painful, and quite different when they're being inflicted on you. I bet the kids you tortured are still in agony."

The tied man's eyes were wide open, looking for any possible escape. The binds were cutting into his wrists and ankles and a leather strap around his neck was slowly strangling him as his legs, which were entangled around the other end, began to tire, and sink towards the floor.

His fingers and toes were getting cold, and he was feeling pins and needles as the blood started to drain from his extremities.

In front of his face three items bounced in to view. Four sharp barbs cut from a barbed wire fence, then a six-inch copper pipe.

"Here's my offer, Chubby. Tell me what I want to know, and I won't shove that pipe up your arse and deposit those barbs deep inside your rectum. Imagine the looks you're going to get in A&E."

His tormentor was chuckling, mocking him.

"I didn't kill the ginger fella, I swear. I only helped him dump the body."

Success!

"So, you dumped him overboard?"

"No, he's in the ballast tank."

He confessed that he had got an old friend called Dovey on the ferry through the staff entrance into the port and on to the ferry with the crew. He thought he was doing an errand for the local paramilitaries.

It was a regular occurrence enabling Loyalist paramilitaries to move to and from the mainland without being manifested.

Dovey knew all about Taylor's lifestyle and had provided him snuff videos and homeless boys from time to time. He later gave the kids back to his supplier for disposal. He never asked where.

Through his sobs he explained that Dove had later approached him on the ferry and told him he was on a mission for the commander of the Rathcoole UVF and ordered him to help. If he had refused it would have been a death sentence.

It was Dove who had offered to show the tall man around the ship with an old friend. The big guy had an interest in engineering, he explained. When they got to the confines of the engine room Dove punched the visitor and kept asking him where one of their ex-friends was.

The guy didn't know or refused to tell so Dove went crazy and hit him with a huge spanner that was hanging on the wall. He then left Taylor to dispose of the body and left with the guy's car keys.

He didn't see Dovey again, though he suspected that he drove the guy's car off the ferry and probably dumped it with Loyalist sympathisers in Scotland.

"Who was he asking for?"

"I can't remember, I was scared in case any of the engineers came in."

A slap with the hot iron quickly refreshed his memory.

"Johnno! He kept asking for Johnno," he screamed.

"Dovey was taking the piss out of him, saying that the guy he was after had been shagging the ginger's wife. There was dark blood and shit coming out of his ears. His skull was deformed."

"So where is the body?" he asked calmly.

"The DB, Double Bottom tanks. I had to undo twenty-three bolts then bump him inside. I'd tightened about a dozen of them back up when I heard the banging."

"Banging? What banging?"

The fat man gulped.

"The guy inside was banging, he wasn't dead, so I put the rest of the bolts back, greased up the spanner to cover the blood and dropped oil on the mess on the floor."

The double bottom of the ship was a safety feature to avoid ingress of water in case of grounding or collision.

These void spaces were used to store ship ballast water to stabilize the ship. Winker's injured body would have eventually succumbed to the blow on his head or hypothermia. The body would then have drifted along the ballast compartment waiting to be found when the ship entered dry dock for a major overhaul.

The fat man felt the bile rise in his throat the split second that Johnno's Aku boot hit him squarely in his unprotected bollocks.

He looked around the room and picked up the paedophile's mobile phone and rang a number he had memorised. His accent was more Gypsy than Irish.

"Crimestoppers? Got a friend of yours here. Get round and speak to Fat Tommy, he has a tale to tell, and search the ballast tanks of the European Causeway." He gave the address and clicked the phone off.

The fat man was crying uncontrollably as he closed the back door.

The Vex Bar, Shankill Road, Belfast

"Are you sure we'll get the contract, Bobby?" the main man asked.

The room was smoky, the Brigadier and Battalion commanders were sitting around a long table. Union and Ulster flags decorated the walls. This was no ordinary UVF Brigade meeting.

'Bobby' Charlton was centre of attention. He had inside information about the future of the four large blocks of flats in Rathcoole.

"It's a done deal and I have a legitimate demolition company to front the scam. They'll be given the job of flattening the Rosslea Way flats, so Monkscoole House and Abbotscoole will be first," he bragged.

Only a year before Charlton had used a similar scheme with a front company to install windows in to the Carncoole and Glencoole blocks on the same complex.

Within the next few months, the Carncoole and Glencoole blocks would be history and Charlton would be looking for a friendly construction firm to front the new regeneration project. It was going to be a very profitable scam.

The Rosslea Way flats scam was a master stoke by Charlton. The inside information provided by Sir John was priceless and allowed him to remain one step ahead of his competitors. As long as he kept Sir John sweet the profits would keep flowing.

The Parker family demolition company was in the lead for the tendering process. The council's contract specification had been leaked to ensure they were ahead of the game.

"Is this the dealings of the Ulster Political Research Group?" another guy shouted.

"The council and the UPRG have decided that regeneration is needed, and we have found the right company that will win the contract," Charlton answered.

The council funding would ultimately be syphoned off along with protection revenue and 'voluntary contributions' from local businesses to source even more drug dealing. Monies received from the city council would be paid to the legitimate company accounts, but then transferred to several different offshore accounts electronically the same day.

At the first sign of danger the company's accounts would be closed, leaving the original legitimate company they used to gain the contract to deal with the fallout.

Glengormley

John Murrey was late for the meeting; he still had the kids to drop off at school and his ears were ringing from his nagging wife. The UDA gathering, he had hosted the night before had gone on a wee bit longer than he had wanted. He now had to get up to Antrim to negotiate with the Gimp with the Limp.

"I'll back the car off the drive, kids," he shouted to the still-open door.

The car started first time and rolled down towards the black tarmac road.

Beneath his seat a small mercury ball rolled backwards, enabling an electrical connection which in turn exploded the silver detonator embedded in five pounds of Enegel Super Dyne explosive stolen from the quarries in Antrim.

The car lifted, then bounced back to earth, rolling back across the road into a parked van on the opposite side.

The explosive fired upwards through the floor and the driver's seat, sending red hot shrapnel up through Murrey's legs and buttocks, severing his limbs and forcing springs and foam from the chair through his arse and into his bowels and lower intestine.

Charlton, 'The Gimp with a Limp', received the news whilst he sipped his first morning coffee.

"Bobby, I hear that the South East Antrim UDA need a new boss," the voice informed him.

He smiled and put the phone back on the table.

"Dovey, get the teams out now and start moving those fuckers out of our houses. I have good protestant families to be moved in. Our Lord and master needs their votes." He put down his phone and began to crack his fingers.

Dove had already briefed the dozen men standing by the roller shutter doors. Their mission was to remove any Catholics, foreigners, or asylum seekers, no matter if they had children or elderly relatives. All had to go west, into the Nationalist enclave.

CHAPTER EIGHT

Shackley Road, Tyldesley

He was sick of the little thing buzzing. Oh, to go back to a world where you couldn't be contacted twenty-four hours a day! It was the ex-wife again, he inwardly groaned. More bad news, he thought.

Johnno had been kicking around his house wondering what to do now he had time on his hands. The clothes he had worn in Ireland were washed, ironed, and arranged neatly back in cupboards and drawers. One plan was to take Fury to the vets and have his stitches removed.

The phone buzzed louder with each passing second.

"Hi."

She was breathless, panicking. "It's, it's...!"

"Calm down, Shaz, spit it out slowly. It's what?" he tried to calm her.

"Jamie, it's Jamie, some Irish bastard has been screaming down the phone at me. They want you to ring Jamie's number right away, no cops or they will cut his ears off."

He felt like he had been kicked in the pit of his stomach.

"OK, love, leave this with me, but I need some time to get something together." He tried to remain composed so that Sharon could calm down.

"WHAT!" She screamed. "Our son has been fucking kidnapped and you want time?"

"Look, Sharon, I'll get him back, I promise, but I need some help from a friend over the water. Ring Jamie's phone and tell them I'm working lates over in Yorkshire, you've left a message and rung my boss. Get me that time…. please"

"Oh my god, the police are here now," she gasped.

"Play dumb and ring me back once they leave."

As soon as the line went dead, he was back on the phone.

"Hendo, I need a massive favour. I need you to triangulate a mobile for me and I need it right now."

He practically leapt up the stairs and entered the back bedroom. The room was his storeroom. Lockers with sturdy padlocks lined the room; under-bed lockers were teeming with different clothes he could use in the street or on rural operations.

He quickly found a small technical tool box with a range of screwdrivers and Allen keys before grabbing his car keys and racing off towards Manchester.

Gorton

He drove slowly around the estate. Damo's spotters were idling in the sunshine, leaning on their BMX bikes, and trying to look menacing at any stranger walking by.

Others were already high after passing around a joint or popping a pill or snorting a line of coke.

Sharon had phoned him back with the details of some suspicious circumstance which had happened at Jamie's college.

His blue Ford Focus had been seen outside the college door with its driver's door open and the engine still running. His sunglasses were on the pavement as if he had left quickly.

Some of the students had reported a black van driving around the area during the morning, two large bald-headed men in the front. Sharon had also seen a similar van that morning.

The police had listed Jamie as missing from home, no mention of a kidnap it was a suspicious occurrence, but with Sharon not providing any further help they had nothing else to help their investigation.

Johnno grabbed the small multi-function screwdriver from the centre console and exited the car.

A bored youth stood nonchalantly at the end of the alleyway which led to the back gate of Damo Francis's home. He watched the white man shuffle towards him and scowled.

"Hey, you, fuckin' smack head. If you're not here to score jog on before I jab, you!" He flashed a large zombie knife to emphasise the warning.

The older man's head was bowed in submission. He slowly closed the space between them. A black baseball cap was pulled low, covering his face. His clothes looked old and scruffy, and his shoes well worn.

"No bother, man, I just need some gear, a quick fix. Help me out, bro."

The boy fiddled into his underwear, searching for a wrap.

The kid was well known to the surveillance team, a young hothead who would do anything for Damo. He had posters of Tupac and The Notorious B.I.G on his bedroom wall. He spoke like a west coast gangster, a Crip, or a Blood; he even had a red bandanna around his neck to show a connection to a gang on the other side of the world.

The man kept walking, then launched his head into the youth's face, then smashed his skull into the brick wall behind him. There was an awful crunch as the skull broke. He dragged the unconscious body further along the alley and dumped it behind a bin.

Carefully he studied the wall until he found the microscopic aperture of the spy camera covering the back exit of the drug dealer's den. He took a piece of masking tape and covered the lens.

Franks was basking in the sun. Johnno looked at him through a hole in the simple wooden gate. He was on a recliner, wearing shorts and smothered in sun cream. Damo Franks sunning himself on the decking, oblivious to the danger facing him. Confident of his own safety by a group of young boys riding around the estate aimlessly on bikes.

Happy to spend on security on his front door, but too stupid to realise that the rear door was the real danger. Johnno had been in the back garden before when he accompanied technical officers wiring the house for sight and sound.

He knew the layout of the property intimately after studying plans before the technical attack.

Damo felt the cold shadow spread across his back. Another fuckin' cloud, he thought, typical Manchester summer.

He began to rise when the cling film wrapped tightly over his face.

Panic: he couldn't breathe, his lungs craved it. A punch hit him in the back of the head followed by a boot in his ribs; he felt them bend then crack. He was dragged by the hair and thrown in through the kitchen door.

He tried to focus through the plastic on the dark-shaped attacker.

The figure calmly walked towards a light fitting and started to touch it.

Johnno had kept his foot in the small of Francis's back whilst he unscrewed the light fitting which acted as the leach power source for the covert cameras and loudspeakers placed throughout the premises.

"You have four minutes till your brain dies and the clock is ticking Bro!" The voice informed him.

Damo stopped struggling.

He was about to pass out when a finger pierced the plastic; cold air was sucked into his burning lungs. He gasped as his hands were thrust behind him and tied tightly.

The black and white kitchen was well kept and clean; a machete hanging on a towel hook was the only thing out of place.

He lifted Damo, speaking slowly to him like he was a child. He touched his thighs with the cold steel of the machete.

"Yo man, you fuckin' diss, me, this be a taxing, Bro. No comebacks or my crew will be taking your head. You don't wanna war on these streets, Bro." Johnno stressed using his best street accent.

He pushed him face-first on to the floor and gave the prone man a sharp kick to his bollocks.

The plastic ripped further as Damo spewed.

"You're a dead guy you blood clot mother fucker!"

"Speak English, Damo, you're from Gorton, not East LA or Kingston, Jamaica."

Johnno quickly made his way upstairs and checked out of the front window. Damo's street soldiers were nowhere to be seen, possibly drifted off to the park for a kick about.

The large queen-sized bed was covered in black silk sheets and a vast number of pillows. A huge mirror covered the ceiling.

He pulled back the zebra skin rug and lifted the trap door beside the bed. In the space was a box filled with bags of white and brown powder, individual bags of dark white crystals. A stack of burner phones, bundles of cash, and two green plastic packages. He lifted the first one and looked inside.

The Glock 19 was compact, it still had grease on the top receiver. The polymer grip felt familiar in his gloved hand. He reached back in the hole and retrieved a box of 9mm ammunition and two empty magazines in plastic wrappers.

The cash was placed in his jacket pocket beside one of the burner phones before he squirted lighter fuel over the bags of white powder, brown powder and white blocks of crack which looked like Kendal mint cake. He struck a match and calmly walked downstairs.

He slapped Damo's arse with the side of the long machete before reconnecting the cameras' power source. Smoke was forming at the upstairs windows as he pulled back the masking tape of the rear camera. He checked the boy by the bin.

He was breathing. Cops would put it down to a gang-on-gang assault and the technicians would put the disturbance down to a power surge at just the wrong time.

Hendo phoned just as he got back to his car.

Jamie's phone was in the area of a disused farm. The phone pinged as the text message landed. Canteen Farm, a vacant farm complex off Rindle Road in Astley Village.

Hendo had also attached a link to a property website. The building and land were being sold for renovation: half a million quid for the seven acres of birchwood land and outbuildings.

There was an old peat plant and mini railway behind the property and Johnno knew the area like the back of his hand.

Whiteabbey, Belfast

"The fuckin' thing won't light," he cussed under his breath.

"Are you sure this is the right shop?" his partner asked.

"Yes, they said the Turkish barbers on the corner, of course it's the right shop."

The rag sticking out of the end of the bottle finally flamed to life and the man ran across the road and launched the missile towards the large plate glass window. The window was constructed from hardened glass and easily defeated the improvised Molotov cocktail.

"Fuck, Dovey will fucking kneecap us if we mess this up!"

They ran across the road and poured the contents of the last remaining bottle through the letterbox of the shop then pushed in the lighted rag. They spied through the aperture as the liquid spread across the floor towards the stairs that caught light with a blinding orange and blue flash.

Rindle Road, Astley Moss

Johnston slowly rolled the van to a stop. He had just crossed a small bridge over a bulrush-lined brook: a tight S bend was to his front. He took out the mini binoculars from his olive colour Paramo jacket and observed the flat farm lands.

Astley Moss was a sparsely populated area of farms and small holdings. The kidnappers had chosen both well and badly. Well because the only law enforcement that ever visited the area was the GMP force helicopter which flew over the fields and peat bogs from its nearby base at Barton Aerodrome, and badly because it was Johnno's back yard.

He had used the area many times to train officers to map read and to conduct covert rural operations. He knew the farmers, drank with them, listened to their gripes.

As he peered across the apex of the S bend, he picked out a line of three small farms set back off the main road which led to the Liverpool to Manchester railway.

The railway line was the oldest in the world and had been the site where George Stevenson had tested 'The Rocket', the first ever steam train. The line and all the buildings were built on special island foundations to prevent them sinking back into the sphagnum moss.

Rail, coal and cotton, the epicentre of the industrial revolution.

After the train line lay a long winding dirt track which interlinked other farms but went nowhere else. It was the biggest cul-de-sac in the area.

Birchwood Farm, Moss Bank, Canteen Farm. He counted them off. Canteen Farm was set back behind a small copse of silver birch trees. A thin grey wisp of smoke slowly drifted from the chimney of the supposedly deserted property. *Absence of the normal, presence of the abnormal.*

The van bumped and groaned as it bounced on its springs down the pot-holed track leading off Rindle Road, the noises and bumps finally easing off as it reached the carefully laid tarmac laid by the farmer down to his home.

A line of vehicles was neatly arranged in the yard. A yellow excavator was chugging away, belching blue-grey diesel fumes into the air; several huge wooden railway sleepers were laid across the front bucket.

A scurry of small hairy terriers barked and fought for his attention. They left dirty paw prints on his cargo pants.

A giant appeared from the corner of the farm; another huge sleeper rested easily on his massive shoulders.

"Ow do, Phil, come to pay your membership fees or are you arranging another daft exercise?" the giant asked as he dumped the wood into the bucket.

Everybody called the giant Sway, a former professional rugby player, slaughterman, and now farmer. He had been given the nickname Sway after his many years working as a lead driller on the North Sea oil rigs. His colleagues commented that even in the strongest ocean gales he would never sway.

Now he was the King Solomon of the area and the steward of the local village club. If the Sway said you were barred, you never came back. If you had a problem with your neighbour, you went to see the Sway. If you needed any building work or advice the Sway was the man to see.

The big man had also played the part of a dangerous criminal during one of Johnno's test exercises. The eight officers had spent hours stalking into a position to observe the big man's daily routine, only for him to find every one of their hiding places within an hour of first light.

Disheartened he opened up the village club to drown their sorrows. They were still there the next morning.

A tall woman appeared from the door of the farmhouse carrying a huge mug of steaming liquid.

"Hi, Phil, kettles on if you want a brew," she asked.

"No thanks, Gill. I just need to talk to the Sway."

"Well, keep your mates out of the club. Took me ages to clean it after that party you had in there. Mess it up again and I'll strangle you."

Phil held his hands up in surrender. He would never divulge that it was her husband who refused to let any of the police officers' leave.

"I take it I'm still in the shit with your missus then?" he asked.

"Always in the shit, just the level that changes," his wise friend pointed out.

"Anything going on down here?"

"No, nothing ever goes on down the Moss – well, apart from somebody mooching around Canteen Farm. It's up for sale but the last few days I've seen a black van going down the lane and a few blokes behind the trees. They might be builders, but I've not heard if the old place has been sold off yet."

The farmers in the area reminded Johnno of their counterparts in South Armagh. Up before dawn, out in the fields all day until dusk. They knew every inch of their property. Every broken branch on a hedge or unusual footprint was noticed and checked.

"By the way, Gill was in Mary's shop this morning and there were two strangers in front of her, big lads. She thought they were travellers, but Mary said they were from the North of Ireland, and she should know, being a Sligo woman."

The tall man looked down at his much smaller friend and laid a huge hand on his shoulder.

"Do you need a lift with anything, Phil?" His ruddy face was emotionless.

"Nothing I can't sort out myself. I need to walk down the old peat line if that's OK with you?"

"I'll warn Jessie off next door in case he gets on the jungle drums, and the shotgun cabinet is open in case you see any… rabbits!"

Johnno nodded, but he had the Glock tucked inside his green jacket and the machete hanging from his belt. He shook the giant's big, calloused hand then walked off towards the peat bog.

Canteen Farm, Astley Moss

It was an area he knew well, and it was a good job, years of peat farming had left deep mud-filled scares which would swallow up an unsuspecting walker. The mark of the old peat train track was three feet above the rest of the land and built on bales of cotton back in the eighteen hundreds. The old small gauge rail lines had long gone, and the path was overgrown.

Johnno walked on the far side of the track with just his head visible to the farmsteads to his right. He stopped every fifteen minutes to observe and listen.

He placed the outside of his foot down first as he cautiously avoided standing on any lose twigs. Ghost walking the army called it, he slowly moved his head from side to side scanning the undergrowth ensuring he didn't disturb any wildlife on the ground or nesting birds.

This was his world, stalking his prey; he had done it since boyhood. Tracking animals, creeping up on them, avoiding their warning senses.

He had also used the same skills to stalk the greatest game of all, man.

The wood to his right started to become denser so he crouched low and darted across the path, taking refuge in the foliage of the trees. He made his approach to the derelict farmhouse at a crouch, then waited.

Smoke, voices, and the sound of chopping alerted him. He watched a man wearing a dark boiler suit struggling with some firewood. He had a black cap on his head which he pulled down as he dragged the wood towards the ramshackle farmhouse.

The walls of the farm were cracked in places, the bare stone poked through. The windows and doors were covered in clear polythene sheets. Slowly he probed in then out of the building like the shape of a flower petal. He had distinctly heard two voices, but no sound of Jamie.

Once satisfied he crawled back to the cover of the wood and used one of the stolen burner phones to call his son's mobile. A gruff Irish voice answered.

"Please don't hurt my son. How much do you want?"

There was a silence as the kidnapper suddenly realised that there was money to be made.

"Fifty grand in an hour or we'll start cutting the boy's fingers off. You have an hour," he commanded.

"Look, I'm at a bird's house in Chester. I need to get you the cash. It'll take me at least two hours."

There was a pause. He could hear a muffled discussion.

"OK, ring me when you're ready and I'll tell you where the exchange will take place. No Peelers or the boy dies." the thug laughed.

"Please don't hurt my boy, I beg you," he sobbed.

The phone went dead. Johnno sat back against a silver birch tree; his crocodile tears gone. He tried to stifle the anger building in his stomach.

He remembered placing his hands on Sharon's bulging bump and speaking to his unborn son, then later feeling him trying to kick his way out of his mother's body. Trips to football, birthday parties, holidays, millions of happy memories. Then the guilt of it should have been more, his overactive libido had driven away from the people he loved the most.

No bully was going to take away his child. He concentrated and subdued the anger; controlled it, channelled it, gave it a focus. Surprise, Speed and Maximum Aggression he remembered from the close quarter battle lessons he had conducted.

He retrieved the Glock from his inside pocket and checked that the small stubby round was correctly seated in the chamber. The brass base shone back at him.

He had spent five minutes stripping down the gun, cleaning off any grease and working the action, even taking time to stop at the deserted area of Pool's Hill to fire off three shots to confirm the weapon was fit for purpose.

He had refilled the magazines, placing the spare in his left coat pocket.

He had no doubts about his other weapon. The machete was razor sharp and had been recently used, judging by the dried blood on the blade.

He checked at his watch then looked at the darkening sky. The wind was getting up and swirling the thin branches above his head. The polythene covering the windows and doors had begun to move and creak.

Cautiously he inched forward through the wood, aiming to peek into the building through the cut in the side door's polythene. A trail of leaves and muddy prints exposed the kidnapper's main entrance.

The ground was soft underfoot, so he moved slowly to prevent any squelching sounds. The branches above his head moved rhythmically and birds were still chirping giving him the confidence that his approach was stealthy.

Inside he heard a voice, a younger voice: Jamie.

From his pocket he retrieved the miniature binoculars. The soft shell of the Paramo jacket prevented any tell-tale rustling which was why he spent such a vast amount of cash on one item. It had proven its worth over the years as he conducted close reconnaissance of targets without ever being compromised.

He refocused until the image became clearer on the hole in the plastic. Inside the men calling themselves McClusky and Freeman were standing beside a plain wooden chair. On the chair was Jamie, tied, bruised but still alive.

His two captors looked like brothers, possibly even twins. He couldn't see anybody else inside.

He reached the last line of trees and hunkered down by the base, eyes fixed on the doorway, which suddenly buckled. A dark shape appeared and followed the line of the wall along, then stood and stopped.

The man stopped, faced the wall, and began to unzip.

Jamie was bound to an old kitchen chair, wrists and ankles bound by thick silver duct tape. A further piece of tape half hung from his left cheek, placed there in case the kidnappers needed to quickly silence him.

His right eye was black and closed, cigarette burns were dotted along both bare arms. The boy shivered in the cold. His position was pushed back against the rear wall well away from the temporary fire which glowed in the opposite corner.

The youth looked up at his hooded captor.

"If I were you, I'd be shitting myself."

"Why do you say that Big Man?" the guy in black scoffed.

"Because my dad will kill you, your family, and anybody that has ever known you." The boy spat out blood.

The captor laughed. "Your Da, the fuckin' dweeb? He was crying on the phone, ya little cunt. Once we've dispatched him and put his head in a box, we'll cut your bollocks off and be home with his fifty grand."

"And when my dad's finished with you it's not over," the youth continued unabated.

"Oh, do tell what's he going to do after my demise?" the man mocked.

"Not my dad, then it's my Mum's turn. She'll dig up your bodies and piss on you both. She hates bullies and you're going to be damned for eternity."

The man belly laughed. "We're Prods, son, we don't believe in that papist clap trap of hell and forever damnation."

Johnno, still at the crouch, carefully made his way towards the man concentrating on pissing up the wall as high as he could. He appeared to be having fun, mesmerised by his skill.

THUNK! The razor-sharp blade hit the pissing man in the nape of his neck, severing the vertebrae from the rest of his spine, almost decapitating him.

The action was so fast that the man appeared to be in a zombie-like trance. He was warm, manoeuvrable. His body was yet to appreciate that it was no longer receiving signals from its brain. It was on auto pilot and still continued to pee.

"Perhaps you need to speak to your god. You're going to be meeting him real soon, probably after a real painful beating," Jamie carried on.

The man backhanded the tethered youth and replaced the tape to gag him.

"You gobby wee fucker, I'm going to kneecap you before I cut you up," he screamed.

The youth looked beyond his aggressor; his eyes fixed in horror at the dark outline of a man leaning against the taught polythene covering the front door. The man's head rested on his right shoulder at an unfeasible, macabre angle.

The captor followed Jamie's horrified stare and saw the zombie. He spun round and reached for a sawn-off shot gun which lay at his feet. Before he could level the weapon at any potential threat a bullet hit him midway up his rib cage, quickly followed by a second shot slightly higher. A third shot hit him below his right eye, taking off his face, which swung like a discarded mask.

"El Presidente!" Johnno whispered as he stepped through the cut in the plastic sheet. A ruffling noise was emanating from beside the fire. A third man was struggling to unzip himself from the big green maggot of the old army sleeping bag.

Johnno made large deliberate strides to avoid the body on the floor and pumped two bullets either side of the besieged man who gawked up with terrified eyes.

"Tell me who sent you and you'll live," he promised.

The prone man looked to his left; an ancient Webley revolver was beside him. The bag's zip suddenly burst as the man's adrenaline surged as he tried to survive.

His head exploded as the bullet hit him in the cranium without him ever touching the rusting heirloom.

The room was still: even Jamie remained quiet in his restraints. Johnno checked the remaining rooms, then ripped the gag from his son.

"Any more?" he whispered.

"No, Dad, there were only three of the fuckers!" the lad gasped.

"Hey, watch your mouth, what would your mother say?" he rebuked.

The boy looked ashamed - which was amazing, seeing that he had just witnessed his dad administer a bloodbath.

"Their van is parked at the back I think, Dad."

Johnno ripped at the thick bindings until his son was free. He tucked the bindings into his pocket to avoid any tell-tale forensics.

He then checked each body for any identification and swiped their mobile phones. From his pocket he retrieved a dark plastic Faraday bag to stop any signals emitting from the communication devices.

All three men were carrying driving licences issued in Northern Ireland. Their addresses were all from the Newtownabbey area. McClusky and Freeman also carried their old identification cards.

"Dad, somebody's coming."

Phil turned his head then, heard a familiar put, put put of a diesel engine rumbling up the track towards the farm.

The machine was dwarfed by the giant seated on top. A dark double-barrelled shotgun lay across his massive thighs.

They walked outside the farm building to greet the Big Sway.

"Evening," he mumbled as he walked towards Johnston and his sibling.

He trailed his left leg slightly due to an arthritic knee.

"Big rabbits?" he exclaimed as he pointed his head towards the still-standing zombie.

"Bit of a misunderstanding," Phil tried to explain.

"Remind me to explain myself fully to you in the future. Our Stacy had rung me this morning, said your boy had been snatched and to put the word out about a black van. I had a feeling you'd be round soon."

The big man walked up to the zombie and picked it up by the waist; the remaining sinews tore away, the head rolling on the floor.

"Gross!" exclaimed the boy.

"Too many video games," the giant said as he picked up the head with a bloody ear and dumped it into the bucket of the excavator, quickly followed by the rest of the body.

"How many more?"

"Two in the farm and a black rental van in the old barn."

The Sway looked at them both, shook Phil's hand and patted the boy on the head.

"I'll clean up here. I take it you don't want anybody else involved. One of the lads will take the tracker from the van and dump it miles away. Oh, you owe me a pint or two now!"

The bodies were dumped in a deep pit and covered in lime in the middle of the peat bog. The weapons and any trace of their existence buried in another hole. Then the derelict Canteen Farm set ablaze.

Twenty minutes later he was back in Sharon's arms, being fussed over like a mother hen.

"Sharon, I need time to sort this out. I'm going to be backwards and forwards between here and the Province. I don't know why these people are looking for me, but I do have a vague idea of the organisation they work for. They're merciless and won't stop until I make them stand down," he lied.

Between them they worked out a credible story that would keep the cops at bay. They rehearsed the tale over and over until Jamie was word perfect.

"I need to go and pack. I'm off to Belfast."

Jamie jumped to his feet and hugged his father like he had never done before. Tears were welling in his eyes. The emotion of the last few hours had begun to take effect.

"Be careful, Dad."

Sharon joined in the hug and whispered in her ex's ear.

"Kill the twats."

Whiteabbey, Belfast

Inspector Evans continued making notes as the fire brigade's incident manager and the local fire investigator compared their findings.

"Arson, again," the investigator stated.

The Inspector rested her pen. "How do you know that?"

"Well, the flame pattern is strange, and you can smell the accelerant even now." He led the party through the shell of the house, then knelt by the corner. He poked around in the ashes and soot until he found a small piece of wax and a smaller piece of rubber.

"The old condom over a candle trick," he explained.

The arsonist had filled a condom with lighter fuel, then suspended the concoction over a burning candle which acted as the timer and detonator. A simple but highly effective method of causing a fire and getting away.

"Well, whoever the guy is, they're not arsonists any more. I have four charred remains upstairs. He's now a murderer."

North Manchester Division, GMP

Johnno was driving down to his meeting when Sharon told him that a female member of the admin staff at the North Manchester Headquarters and her partner had been arrested and cautioned for unauthorised access to his personnel file.

The member of staff had been working from home due to an ongoing medical condition. She used a GMP laptop and was believed to be completely trustworthy.

During her first interview she had sobbed that she had no idea about accessing any personnel files. The officers questioning her showed her a list of times when the files had been accessed.

It was when she claimed she was asleep after taking her medication that the officers began taking an interest in her partner.

Her boyfriend was a Police Community Support Officer, she claimed he stayed downstairs playing video games when she went to bed. She had allowed him to use her laptop to sign on and off the Force Duty Management System. It helped him pinch a few minutes off his shift or grab a little more overtime on his flexi sheet.

After enquiries with PSNI the Detectives discovered that PCSO Alan McNair was a Northern Irishmen, born and raised in a place called Whiteabbey! They confirmed that he was formally a member of the Young Protestant Volunteers. He had left Ulster to escape the paramilitaries.

An evidence bag was placed on the table immediately the interview started with McNair. In the bag was a tiny phone, a Zanco, one of the smallest in the world. It looked like a toy or a spy device.

"Some guys in Ulster wanted to get in touch with an old soldier friend, invite him to a party, they told me," he blurted out.

The investigators then placed down an itemised call list; three calls made to another mobile. The timings matched the time that Phillip Johnston's P File had been accessed.

"I had to do it," he wept. "Why do you think I came to Manchester? I had to escape. My family are still over there, still in danger. They said they'd burn them out if I didn't help them."

"Who did you speak to?"

"I don't know, but he's South East Antrim UVF and he had an English accent."

Rathcoole

Dove walked into Charlton's office and slumped into the fake leather chair opposite the boss's desk. Charlton looked at him, waiting for an explanation.

"Bobby, I can't get hold of the Harpers. They snatched his boy as ordered, then nothing."

"No news reports?" Charlton asked.

"Fuck all. I've lost my old army buddy; the Manchester cop I was using has been lifted and now the Harpers go AWOL. I think Johnston has taken them out."

Charlton's bifocals moved to the end of his long nose. He cracked his fingers nervously.

"I fuckin' grew up with the Harpers' father, carried his coffin with them. If anything has happened to them, I'll…!" He was flying into a rage.

"You'll do what? He's in the wind now. He's probably on to us and that's frightening. Who knows just what assists he has over here."

"Get the man on it and find out more about his Irish bird, the Peeler. Round her up."

"What about the guy in prison, the one that blabbed about the murder? He might have turned Queen's evidence on us," Dove reminded him.

"Well, his old cellmate is no longer going to talk, thanks to the Harpers, so make arrangements for him to stay silent as well."

HMP Long Lartin

After showing his passport it took about thirty minutes to move along the process of being searched, having a photograph taken and a dog sniff his balls.

He watched as the Prison Officers unlocked doors and heavy gates. The doors had no handles, just thick brass locks. Some had one keyhole, others two. A twenty-foot Parkhurst prison fence with tiny holes to stop climbers lined the outdoor walkway.

He finally entered the visits hall to find Sampey wearing a red bib over his grey tracksuit, sitting on a green plastic chair on the far side of a small grey coffee table.

His former colleague gave him a wry smile and shook his hand.

"Sergeant Phillip 'Johnno' Johnston, as I live and breathe. When they told me I had a visitor I had no idea it would be a Protestant baby murderer!"

Phil looked at him disbelievingly. "Protestant Baby Murderer? What meds have they got you on, Samps?"

"I saw the light, an epiphany, you might say. Catholicism is more than a religion; it's a political power. Therefore, I'm led to believe there will be no peace in Ireland until the Catholic church is crushed."

"Let me guess: the words of your new hero, Oliver Cromwell."

"He was a visionary, doing the work of the Lord."

"Nothing to do with being bagged up in a high security prison, fed on the best mind-bending drugs money can buy and then rubbing shoulders with the dregs of society. I like the scar as well. Game of mummies and daddies get a bit rough?" he taunted.

"The British Army killed Loyalist men, woman, and children during the Troubles, and they continue to do so, wherever they deploy. It's a fact."

"A fact which you can't evidence, I suppose. Just throw up a lot of shit, hearsay, and shout louder than any other fucker. What the fuck happened to you? You started acting funny after the forced crash during Recompense."

"Recompense, well that's a word I haven't heard in a while."

"But you have talked about it. I know you have."

Sampey looked towards the corner. Some of the female visitors were buying items from the small family tuck shop. Phil went over and bought two cans of Fanta.

There were about twenty other families in the visitors' hall. Babies were crying and toddlers not being cradled in their fathers' arms were running around or engaged in the play area.

The prisoner had put weight on, the grey tracksuit bottoms and a grey Under Armour T Shirt were tight. The L-shaped dull red scar along his left cheek was present from a Republican prisoner.

He handed over the can and waited while Sampey took a massive gulp.

"Why were we fighting the Loyalists? They were on our side: we should have been arming them against the Papists."

"They were terrorists, Samps, they killed innocent people the same as the Republicans. Now all of your new friends are murderers and drugs dealers. Not the best role models in the community, I would argue."

"Good people defending their communities from the growing threat from the Nationalists. Have you seen the demands that Sinn Fein are making?"

"Bollocks, they're just drug dealing bullies looking after their own bank accounts. A radical Presbyterian, is that what you've become? You probably don't see the real news from the Province. They call it an 'acceptable level of violence'."

Sampey shook his head as Phil recounted the current assaults happening on the Loyalist estates. Families excluded, asylum seekers beaten, and businesses burnt to the ground. The death count was rising, more sectarian attacks were being carried out as the Loyalist high command tried to draw the Nationalists into a fight, a return to the gun.

PSNI resources were at breaking point as they tried to reduce the onslaught.

"You murdered that young kid that was trying to surrender, Phil. You then tried to kill me, you bastard."

"Wow, that bang on your head was worse than I thought. The lad was shot by one of his own, the bullet passed through him and hit you. Look at the forensic reports, look at our statements, for fuck's sake, re-read your own statement."

"I started getting the headaches after that job, fucked me up. I still can smell the flesh of the driver as he burned."

Phil slowly went through the events of the night, trying to pull each element and make Sampey reflect on each fragment.

"You were going forward to arrest the kid when he was shot from behind. Parts of his throat were on your overalls. The bullet hit the chest plate of your body armour. It knocked you over. I lifted you up - remember?"

Tears were rolling down Sampey's face as he relived the night.

"They said his dad wanted to know what happened, just to get some peace, so I told them."

"You told them your twisted version of events; you were probably suffering with concussion. Over the years you have convinced yourself that your version is the truth when it's not. A lot of people are in danger because of you talking to these fuckwits."

"Do you know who the boy's dad is?"

"Does it matter?"

"He's a top jockey, a Loyalist politician, Sir John Smythe. My old pad mate was called Corbishley. He's the second in command in the South East Antrim UVF 'Bobby' Charlton is his boss. He was in for armed robbery after leaving he Province, but I think he's gone back to start the war again."

Johnno took a sip of his Fanta and smiled at his old team mate.

"I'm afraid not, Samps because 'the Gimp with a Limp' had him thrown out of a high building without a parachute. So, no ethnic cleansing from your old mucker, but he was trying to sell his story to the security forces who also employ your hero, Mr Charlton."

"Your lying Johnno, I know because your lips are moving. The way you lied to all the women that were in your bed."

Johnston smiled at his old team mate.

"You know I'm not lying, that scumbag and all his followers are clearing the decks to stop any shit falling back of them. Stay safe Samps and watch your back."

House of Lords Rest Room

The four old men sat around the grandiose Peers' dining room, sipping coffee. They were pillars of the state: a former Admiral, two life peers and an ex Liberal Democrat. The mood was conspiratorial.

"Gentlemen, we have a problem. I have just been on the phone to our supplier and there is trouble afoot."

All of the men had been given top of the range encrypted smart phones. The EncroChat device gave them the ability to communicate covertly, arrange secret rendezvous and arrange payments and favours.

No GPS, camera, or microphone to enhance privacy, devices were sold with pre-installed applications, one being EncroChat, an off the record-based messaging application which routed conversations through a central server based in France.

The handset was switched on by pressing the power button together with the volume button; the phone booted to a secret, encrypted partition which facilitated secret communication via the French servers.

They had chosen the code names Green Seat, Orange Seat, Red Seat and Blue Seat as their user profiles.

Every six months a delightful messenger would arrive and hand over newly encrypted devices.

"There has been a problem with the supply chain. I'm afraid that this weekend's gathering at the Manor has been postponed until they sort out the matter." Green Seat explained.

Faces of former members of the house glared at them from the walls of the dimly lit room. Red Seat squirmed on his ox blood red leather dining chair. A gold embossed portcullis was in the centre of the chair's back rest, and it felt like it was burning through his spine.

"Is there anything we can do to help our friends in Ulster?" he asked.

"The Knighted Loyalist said it's probably better that we let the dust settle on this matter. God, forbid we have another Kincora type incident. I don't think the house could withstand another enquiry. The great unwashed in society want rid of us. Let's not feed the fire."

Blue Seat carefully placed down his coffee cup. There was a slight tremor in his hand.

"We no longer have the protection from our friends in the establishment. There will be no help to cover up any scandal if, as my learned friend is alluding to, the brown stuff hits the proverbial fan."

Whiteabbey, Belfast

The young man was sweating madly. He had been chased over the estate, his pursuers on bikes, cars, and foot.

He had received a beating for running now he was going to get his main punishment for committing the heinous crime of not turning up for a UVF event and then not paying a fifty pound fine for non-attendance.

The fine had risen weekly and now reached the princely sum of two hundred quid. Now he was laying on the concrete floor of a half-built house surrounded by men dressed in black.

His shoulders were in agony due to the weight of the man standing on his shoulders. His arms and legs were being stood on by the crowd. The weight was crushing his bones.

A light shone in his face as the man on his shoulders rambled on about discipline and punishment.

The man was small in stature, but the black balaclava and the large grey breeze block he held in both hands above his head gave him the look of a monster.

He stopped, then slammed the breeze block into the hapless man's face.

There was a sickening thud. Some tried to hide their eyes, others marvelled at the brutality of the event.

The man stepped off the victim's shoulders and aimed a kick into his unprotected jaw.

"Let that be a lesson to all of you. If you're told to turn up to an event you get there or face the consequences. Next one will get this."

From beneath his black nylon bomber jacket, he exposed the handle of a 9mm Browning automatic pistol.

Shackley Road, Tyldesley

The back bedroom was an untidy mess, Clothing was spread out over the floor and boxes of equipment laid out on the bed as Johnno assessed the merit of taking each item.

A large rucksack with its mouth gaping open sat beside the bed waiting to be filled. A smaller black daysack lay beside it.

A thick camouflaged all in one suit covered in waterproof Gore-Tex was folded up ready for packing. The suit had been issued to Special Forces units for High Altitude High Opening insertions behind enemy lines; however, they were soon in great demand for the observation teams lying in the cold for days and weeks.

A Garmin smartwatch and Spyderco serrated lock knife were tied together by paracord.

In the daysack he loaded a digital SLR camera and three different sized lenses with an assortment of stands. He checked then loaded a hacking kit and Leatherman multi-tool which could fix a laptop to a Land Rover.

In a small black leather pouch, he checked his lock picks, three-piece seven pin kit. They were Southard style lock picks, hooks, rakes, double-sided wafers, tension wrenches. He had learnt the lock picking craft as part of his methods of entry course and had become much in demand due to his technical skills.

He packed and repacked, removed and changed items until he was happy that he had everything he needed for the task. After packing the bags into his car, he set off back to the ferry.

Parker's Ground Works, Co Antrim

The large wooden box was placed in the centre of the portacabin floor, and the lid opened. There were pink and orange sausages on one side, small black plastic boxes arranged neatly on the other and two large rolls of cord which looked like the biggest washing line in the world.

Dove knelt down and started unpacking the items, emphasising every piece to the gathered audience as if they were children.

He laid out four different coloured sausages on the floor: pink, orange, blue and purple.

"This is Enegel, high explosive. This is Toe Blast, then Super Gel, Super Dyne and finally Super Enegel." He then threw a sausage at each man and giggled as they desperately grabbed the flying colours before it hit the floor and exploded.

"It's not dangerous, for god's sake. You can throw this stuff on the fire, and it won't go bang. It needs something to make it reach critical mass – then, boom."

The audience didn't appear to trust the detail in his lecture.

He opened up one of the small plastic boxes. Inside were six small silver tubes with wires attached to the end.

"Now these little bastards are dangerous. Electrical detonators are very susceptible to being banged about or changes in temperature. I was on a course in the army when one of these things blew our instructor's fingers off, so be careful."

The pupils shuffled nervously in their seats.

He finally took out one of the reels.

"This is detonating cord. You attach this into the Enegel and then put a detonator on the cord to make up your explosive chain. The det goes bang, the cord burns and that sets off the bang at the end."

One of the students raised his hand.

"That stuff burns, Dovey?"

The Brummie laughed. "Yes, it burns at four miles a second, so don't be stood over it when it goes off or your legs and bollocks will disappear."

Thomas Parker sat back, trying to hide a smile. He was an experienced demolitions officer, with years of experience in carefully dropping any structure from a tree to a large building, often without resorting to using plastic explosive. He looked at Dove and his men, trying to think of a way to get them off his back.

He cautiously peered into the box to look at the remaining contents. There was a fine grey dust covering the other items.

Salt, Thomas immediately thought.

"Here, Thomas, all this stuff is yours now, and there's plenty more if you need it. Keep it off the books and keep the price down." Dove marched his men out of the office.

'Muppets,' Parker thought. His chosen demolition party was a handpicked bunch of idiots chosen only because of their ability to turn up on time to UVF meetings.

They would probably blow themselves up rather than a decrepit tower block. How the hell did he get into this mess.

"God help me!" Parker cried.

CHAPTER NINE

Seahill, Northern Ireland

They had slept in late. Johnno was standing at the upstairs window of her house, looking out across the water. On the other side were the dark hills of South East Antrim, and the towns of Newtownabbey, Rathcoole, and Carrickfergus.

He took a sip from the steaming coffee cup and looked around the room. The word minimalist sprung to mind. A picture of an older couple, mother, and father perhaps, then another picture of the same couple many years before, hair darker fewer wrinkles.

A picture of a man wearing the green uniform of the RUC, the old police force before the move to PSNI. A young man, a happy man. There was a rose by the picture frame.

"That's my brother, Derek," she spoke.

He didn't hear her tiptoe into the room.

"Is he still with PSNI?"

"Only in spirit. He was shot on his own doorstep five years ago. His son witnessed everything. Two men wearing 'Scream' face masks."

Flusky was filling up as she went through the details.

Her brother was a Detective Sergeant working with the Organised Crime Unit. He had been investigating a drugs gang in Rathcoole. During his research he had uncovered links with children's homes and charity organisations supporting orphans. Some members of his squad had told him to drop the case, but that wasn't Derek's way.

He had found a booby trap bomb under his car and his wife and children had been approached by intimidating men in the street. Their message was clear: stop the investigation.

On a drunken night out with PSNI Officers Phil had been told the urban myth that nobody should ever reopen the Billy Wright murder, or the Pat Finucane assassination never ask why John Stalker's office was burned down and certainly never even mention the

Kincora Boys home. All of the cases were bad juju and needed to be avoided.

Their afternoon run along the coast to Grey Point Fort then down on to Crawfordsburn beach had been enjoyable, especially when she sprinted off up the hills, the tight lycra of her shorts showing off her petite arse.

After showering together, he laid out the rucksack and daysack, then began to unload everything. She sat cross-legged on the settee as the floor began to fill with equipment.

They white gusset of her lace panties were proving to be a huge distraction to Phil's attempt to repack his operational grab bag.

They had first met on a Methods of Entry course run by the Security Services and Special Forces. Johnno was one of the instructors and pushed her to the limit.

After the teaching phase the pressure was put on the students as the time between exercises was cut shorter. Less time to plan, less time to recce, less time to brief - and no time to sleep.

The culmination of the exercise was to break into a house and deploy several listening devices. The house was already covered with an array of covert cameras to assess the students' every move and mistake.

Her entry went well: quickly picking the door lock, then finding the dry pasta hidden under the mat, but none of her team were quick enough to catch the cat which bolted out of the premises as they took pictures of the patten in which the penne had been laid out.

She dutifully carried out her task whilst two members of the entry team searched the area to recover Mr Tiddles. As the clock was ticking down, they threw the errant moggy inside and photographed the scene, leaving everything the way they had found it.

The team were all jubilant at the debrief until the first slide came up on the screen. A split picture with Mr Tiddles on the left and a feral tom cat on the right with the caption, 'Spot the difference.'

He had also been her instructor on the surveillance course when their relationship had blossomed. She was good, in fact excellent, at everything she did: motivated, determined, and enthusiastic.

"What's all this gear?" she asked.

"Surveillance has moved on a notch or two. I keep my old military contacts to keep abreast of any new technology. I've managed to get some of my team on courses with my old mob and scrounged some of their old kit."

For years the process of conducting a technical attack had been long and laborious. After getting the necessary authorisation a ground recce was needed to identify and photograph the vehicle to be approached.

A surrogate vehicle would then be located so that entries could be tested and timed. Once inside, the technicians would locate the best place to conceal microphones and power supplies. It was only then that they would sit down with the senior management team to get the final thumbs up to attack the vehicle.

Modern cars were different, however: most had six to eight microchips which controlled speakers, GPS, and external cameras. Car hacking devices could cost as little as twenty pounds and were easy to use. You Tube had thousands of 'How to hack a car' videos.

Johnno had recently been on a group chat with other like-minded individuals who had technically attacked the latest batch of high-end luxury vehicles that now boasted up to twelve microchips which regulated everything from cruise control, safety features and in-car climate settings.

Cars were now just large computers on wheels: they stored travel and call information on the cloud. The latest generation of cars was controlled via cell sites on GSM networks, door locks were opened electronically and in theory hackers could take over the controls of a car to generate an accident.

The hacker could switch on parking cameras to act as a mobile surveillance platform or switch off lights whilst driving in the dark or use the brake lights to indicate the vehicle's current position.

HMP Maghaberry, Lisburn

The grey high security prison housed adult male long-term sentenced and remanded prisoners in both separated and integrated conditions. The population of nine hundred and seventy witnessed suicides, clashes between inmates and prison staff on a daily basis.

Taylor jumped as the big heavy metal gate closed behind him with a resounding clang. He carried a clear bag with the worldly possessions he had gathered whilst in prison.

His remand hadn't come too soon. Unlike sex offenders on the mainland, paedophiles were classed as ordinary criminals and shared the same wings as thieves, arsonists, and murderers.

A large white wrap bandage was covering a scalding attack when a fellow inmate had poured boiling water and sugar over his left arm. During the last few weeks, he had been boiled, eaten shit and been spider manned, in which another prisoner had thrown sperm in his face.

A man was leaning against a dark saloon in the car park opposite the prison gates. He wore dark sunglasses and downturned smile.

He waved at Taylor as he walked towards the roundabout.

"Hi, Joey," Taylor said, a little apprehensive.

"The Boss thought you might need a lift back to Larne, so you'd better get in."

"How did you know I was getting out? I didn't tell anyone. And I've told them nothing, I swear, Joey."

Taylor complied and got into the rear seats. Tears were rolling down his cheeks as the door slammed shut.

Carriages Bistro, Larne

It was a strange feeling dawning on him. He'd had it ever since he drove on to the ferry. He felt like everybody was looking at him. He reflected on the last sentence that the old lady had said to him:

" Trust nobody, not even the police."

He'd phoned Greg to arrange the meeting, but the officer seemed reticent about getting together, but not surprised that he was back in the province.

His car was left on the far side of town in a nondescript street, and he had taken a circular route to the meeting. He wore thick glasses, a cap with a pony tail sticking out, he had hunched his shoulders and changed his usual brisk walk into a shuffle.

He saw them from a distance, Tweddle Dee and Tweddle Dumb, like two peas in a pod. Shaved heads, dark glasses, muscle shirts over biceps that were too big for their arms: a product of chemistry, rather than hard work in a gym.

"Is that the fucker?" the passenger pointed out after looking at the picture on his phone.

"Him? Ya dumb fuck! Nah, our guy is taller and fit. He's just an old tramp," the driver scoffed.

"The boss said he's done the Harpers in, so we need to be careful when we spot him." They simultaneously shrank a little lower in their seats in a poor attempt to avoid observation.

Johnno squeezed on to one of the red bench train seats in Carriages. The bistro was laid out in the shape of an American continental train. Opposite him sat Greg, already looking at the menu.

"The Godfather Pizza is a classic," he recommended.

"Just a tea for me. I'm on my way to Belfast."

Greg ordered and looked around the clientele before he got down to business. His tone was hushed.

"They found Taylor late last night. He'd had a bit of a hammering - literally it looked. The SOCO recons said he'd been in a romper room for about twelve hours and subjected to a horrific beating. Blow torch, pliers, and lump hammers. You get the picture. I've sent the details to DCI Wood on the mainland."

Taylor had been free for less than 24 hours when his naked body was discovered by the side of the Mullaghsandall Road.

"CCTV from Maghaberry shows him being picked up by a guy and driven off. The car was on dummy plates and the guy must have been wearing a disguise or a clean skin because nobody recognises him."

"So, somebody thought that Taylor was a loose end."

"That's the line of enquiry they're going on. He never said anything during his arrest interviews. I went down to interview him at Maghaberry on a legal visit. I got the feeling that he had a lot of dirt on the local paramilitaries and on their links to the ferry, but there was no way he was ever going to blab. One interesting point though. DNA from the skin found on the iron was linked to a young boy who was found strangled on the mainland."

"The mainland?"

"The Met are sending the file over. They said he was a rent boy."

Greg's pizza arrived. He looked tired. Farming and policing: a strange mix Johnno thought.

"Do you know a guy called John Smythe?"

Greg looked at his fingers, sticky with cheese and tomato sauce.

"Sir John Smythe? Yeah, everybody knows him. Good fella. Does a lot for the local community. Why?"

"His name came up in a conversation, I thought he might be linked to the paramilitaries."

Greg scoffed and threw the crust of his pizza back on to the plate. "Nah, mate, you're barking up the wrong tree with that one. He will speak and negotiate with them, but active, no way."

Johnno got the feeling that there was something else. He couldn't put his finger on it.

"If you're still looking for Dove, I've heard that he now frequents the Fern Lodge, Rathcoole. Nice little bar if you like a bit of aggro with your beer," he chortled.

"Did you know Flusky's brother, Derek?"

The question took the smile off the detective's face.

"Yeah, good lad. I worked on his murder, but it was unsolved in the end. No witnesses."

"What about the ballistics report?"

"9mm Browning, been used on a few other shootings. It's linked to the UVF."

"So why did a Loyalist organisation murder a Protestant cop? What was he investigating - drugs by any chance?"

The seasoned Detective rubbed at a tomato stain on his shirt.

"Look, when I first went over to Special Branch, I was told that there are certain cases that shouldn't be reopened or even spoken about."

"The urban myths, and what case was Derek asking about?"

"You're on dangerous ground, Mister Johnston. My advice to you would be to go back home. Leave this to the PSNI. You're not doing Claire any favours including her in your little investigation."

"Is that a warning or a threat?"

Greg rubbed his now-sweaty hands together and immediately left the diner, leaving Johnno scratching his head.

Johnno paid his bill and ducked out on to the street. Tweddle Dee and Tweddle Dumb were still sitting low down in their car with the sun shining off their bald heads, looking at passers-by.

He assumed his huddled walk and slowly made his way back to his car.

The Royal Oak, Green Street

The Royal Oak was conveniently situated next to the PSNI Station on the busy Green Street. It overlooked the ships and planes on and above the lough heading to Belfast.

The pub looked very modern on the outside with silver signage and white walls with the large windows painted pink around the edges.

Sir John took his usual glass of port and brandy from the bar and sat down next to Charlton, He had been on the phone to the Lords and looked worried. His face was as red as the walls. He had walked down from his MP's surgery which was just a few doors along Green Street.

A woman was seated alone at the bar looking at a mobile phone, a small clutch bag lay on the bar. She looked skinny, her brown hair in a pony tail.

He cleared his throat before speaking and looked around to ensure there was nobody in the vicinity to eavesdrop. He looked towards the woman, who remained engrossed in her phone.

"My friends in London are rather vexed at the situation, Mr Charlton. They use your services due to your discretion. Words like compromise and danger do not sit well with them. Do you understand?"

Charlton made an involuntary rub of his bad leg.

"Look, Sir John, any trafficking in this present climate is asking for trouble, and I might point out that this is trouble brought on by you. The fly in the ointment is the fuckin' Brit soldier that murdered your son. He's now been alerted to our friend Mr Dove and his part of the operation."

"Then shut it down, all of it. Don't give him anything to go on."

"Sir John, Dove has been loyal to you and the Unionist Commission."

"Get rid of him, his drivers, and all of his network. You can rebuild it when the heat dies down. Put another team on the soldier. You can take him out in a few months when he thinks everything has gone away."

Charlton looked up at the ceiling. Dove had worked well for him. Yes, he could be a little over zealous at times, but he acted as a good firewall for the other activities carried out by the UVF.

Loyalists Against Drugs had killed or maimed many dealers along the Antrim coast, most of whom had not been authorised to do business in area by the local UVF commander, a certain Mr Charlton.

Dove had also set up the links with a Dublin based cartel to supply drugs and weapons in multi kilo shipments. He was also the kingpin in the 'supply' of vulnerable young boys to certain men of influence on the mainland.

Sir John emptied his glass and stood up, nodding to Charlton as he walked up to the woman at the bar.

"Hello, young lady. My name is Sir John Smythe, the local Member of Parliament. Are you one of my constituents?" He held out a limp-wristed hand which she took.

"Oh, Sir John, what a pleasure," she gushed whilst fluttering her long dark eyelashes.

"I'm new up here, I'm afraid. The council moved me after problems with my other half, the bastard - if you pardon my French, Sir John."

He smiled weakly.

"A victim of domestic violence, my dear? It is the scourge of our society, a veritable plague." He rummaged in his waistcoat pocket and retrieved a card.

"My dear, please give me a call if you require my services." He then kissed the back of her hand, his wet whiskers leaving a whiff of port and brandy.

Johnno watched Sir John leave the bar and walk back past the police station. He had his ear pressed against a mobile phone. Johnno studied the device through his binoculars.

"Why has a politician got an EncroChat phone?" he thought.

EncroChat phones provided 'PGP' - Pretty Good Privacy - but at two thousand pounds for a six-month contract they didn't come cheap. They had quickly become the must-have items for all leading criminal organisations, with over sixty thousand devices sold.

The devices carried a VQ Aquarius X2 Dutch sim card, and all messages were relayed via French domain servers. The phones had no GPS or cameras for law enforcement agencies to exploit.

Each device also had a "Kill Pill Message" to stop all messages and completely wipe the phone if a compromise was suspected. Police forces had reacted by immediately putting all phones in a Faraday pouch to stop criminals killing the phones remotely.

Unbeknownst to the criminal fraternity the system had been hacked by the intelligence community on behalf of law enforcement agencies. The British National Crime Squad had quickly set up Operation Venetic and began to analyse and exploit the deluge of intelligence coming in to their headquarters.

Sir John took a key fob from the pocket of his blue pinstriped suit and pointed it towards a black 4X4 vehicle parked outside his surgery.

The expected light flash did not occur, so he pointed and fired again, This time all lights flashed in acknowledgement.

The first binary coded signal had been picked up by the universal radio hacker and detection device attached to Johnno's laptop. He had already carried out internet checks of car specifications on the cars on the street to identify how many microchips were placed in each vehicle, their locations, and functions.

The stolen code was logged into the laptop to be used at a later date. Using the cursor, he checked the Roll Jam menu and noted that the 4x4 car used Manchester encoding and only took one key press to open the car doors.

He rummaged through a bag of sim cards until he found the one, he was looking for. It took less than five minutes to re-programme the tiny device.

After a quick check to see if the car and sim card were compatible, he left his car and walked along the pavement towards the target vehicle.

Sir John was safely back in his constituency office and the street free from and pedestrians. He carefully scanned up and down the highway.

His street theatre was simple but well-rehearsed. He hit a key on his laptop, which sent the rogue signal to open the doors.

The car's memory immediately told itself that the code was out of sequence when compared to its last command; however, due to the manufacturer's protocols the brain was told to override that anomaly and comply with the command.

The doors clicked open. Johnno ducked as if tying a shoe lace and entered the car, quickly opening a small compartment beneath the dashboard and replacing the sim card.

The whole action took less than thirty seconds. He checked he had not left any tell-tale marks before closing the door and reappearing at the boot of the vehicle and walking away.

She waited five minutes till she joined him.

"I swear that guy is a creep - dirty wee bastard."

She fished inside her bag and produced the pen drive which had been clipped into a covert recording device aimed at the conversation between Smythe and Charlton. Johnno had fitted the powerful covert omnidirectional microphone into her small clutch bag.

He clipped the pen drive into his laptop, and they sat back and listened to the conspirators talk about the future demise of Dove.

"And what did you get up to whilst I was being ogled by the friggin' pervert?" Flusky asked.

"Me? Nothing much. I hacked his car and downloaded the travel data. When he's not in parliament he spends his time driving between his surgery, his home which looks like it's just outside a small village called Straid, and a house in Whiteabbey. So, I suggest you change from your battered wife disguise to top surveillance operator mode."

Graymount Estate, Belfast

The two thugs looked at each. The leader looked again at the address on his phone.

"Are you sure this is the right address, Winny?" his partner asked.

"Look, the boss is never wrong. If he says Fenians are in the house they'll be there. Now get your gun and the can of petrol."

The house at the end of the cul-de-sac appeared to be deserted. White paint was peeling from the walls. The Sky dish was old and rusty. The only new thing was a black transit van parked on the driveway.

"Who the fuck are they?"

"The clerk at the housing office reckons they're the McCreesh family, formally of Turf Lodge. More toasted Taigs tonight."

They walked up the drive, Winny opening the letter box while his partner began to pour the petrol through the aperture.

Neither heard the rear doors of the van opening and the approach of four men dressed in black.

Winny felt the cold steel of the pistol in his ear.

"John Winifred, I presume. I am arresting you for crimes against the Catholic community. As for your friend, Samuel Lamb – well, let's just give you a demonstration."

The door of the abandoned house opened from the inside and both men were ushered in. Winny watched his friend nail gunned to the floor then mercilessly beaten with baseball bats, then covered in the petrol.

The attackers were experts at dealing out a punishment beating. No hits to the head or neck. Winny heard arm, leg and rib bones break in between his friends screams.

With his arms and legs nailed to the floor it was impossible to escape the beating.

The men then marched Winny out to the waiting van.

"You're the lucky one. Ma wants to talk to you. As for your friend, it looks like he's going to a Lamb barbecue."

A hood was put on his head, but he felt a scorch wave on his body, then heard his friend screaming as he burned alive.

Whitehouse Park, Whiteabbey

The large white house was surrounded by an equally large white wall, The black metal security gate was controlled by cameras and had a key-coded lock. Three cars had departed and two arrived in the short space of time they had been watching the entrance.

"Knocking shop, definitely," he proclaimed.

"How do you know? Is this the type of establishment you frequent in your spare time?" she teased.

"It's obvious. Look at the cars - all top of the range, being driven by single men from mid-thirties to sixty," he pointed out.

Another car arrived, a large black 4x4.

"I've been expecting this one, it's been on my tracker since it left the parking space outside the MP's surgery. Perhaps he was going to offer you a job here, Flusky!"

She punched him on the arm.

"We'll leave him here. Who knows how long he might last - five minutes or five hours," he joked as he put the car into gear and drove off.

Straid, Co Antrim

The tracker had picked up movement from the brothel about an hour later and led them to a large fenced-off mansion outside the village of Straid in Co Antrim. Using his binoculars, he surveyed the property with its double garage and neat lawns and flower beds off the Seskin Road.

The house had panoramic views overlooking the Ballyboley Forest on the far side of the valley and rolling manicured farm land.

They sat at a table in the Hub pizza and coffee shop in Straid, which was a small village three miles east of Ballyclare.

"So why are you so interested in Sir John? On the recording Charlton said his was son killed by a Brit soldier - was that you?"

Over the meal he told her about the events of the night in Belfast when Sir John's son was shot by a survivor running for his life. He decided not to mention that the survivor was Charlton.

"Do you know about the case your brother was working on before he was murdered?" he asked.

She thought back to their last conversations. She had been busy with her surveillance team whilst he had been detecting major crimes in Antrim.

They had met up at family gatherings but hardly discussed the job. She believed he was working on a major drug bust as he had mentioned shipments to the mainland.

He also had an interest in a historic case which centred around the Kincora boys' home in Belfast.

Their late father had worked on the case and become frustrated by attempts of Special Branch and MI5 to scupper any investigation into allegations that serious child sexual abuse took place at the establishment.

A strand of intelligence also suggested that boys were trafficked to the mainland to be abused by a paedophile ring with the collusion of the intelligence services.

"The trafficking that Sir John and Charlton spoke about, you don't suppose that could be human trafficking, do you?" she asked.

He rubbed his chin and thought long and hard.

"I really don't know, but I do know a man that does: Dave Dove, and I aim to ask him that very question."

Woodburn Presbyterian Church

The car park of the Woodburn church had been a good point to lay up after another drive past Sir John's address.

The church, which dated back to 1865, was painted in a brilliant white colour which appeared to be doubly bright in the sweltering sunshine.

They were parked at the back of the large grey area which was at the side of the church hall. There was very little traffic on the road, the occasional car, and the not so occasional farm vehicle.

It was mid-afternoon when the first flatbed lorry laden with wooden pallets drove past, quickly followed by a second, then a third.

A heat haze was rising from the tarmac. Flusky heard each lorry slow down, then the metallic creak of a large gate being opened. She remembered the dirt track on the other side of the church.

There was a large 'Keep Out' sign in yellow on the metal barrier across the track which appeared to lead towards a thickly wooded area a few kilometres behind the church.

The rough gravel track appeared well-used. They both watched the dust trails as the three vehicles disappeared into the trees.

Both Flusky and Johnno were sitting back in their seats, looking through the bottom of the windscreen. It was a hot day and they both sweltered on the leather.

A large white Ford van with a 'Fast Move' sign appeared. The driver was a short man wearing a baseball cap. Johnno thought that it could possibly be Dove, but it certainly wasn't a positive identification due to the speed of the van and the distance.

Brake lights flashed as the vehicle slowed. Seconds later another dust cloud appeared as it also raced towards the woods.

They both looked at each other. What the hell was hidden in those trees?

The Fern Lodge, Rathcoole

"Time to start shaking the tree." He commented to Flusky as he exited the car.

The long black fence had large white stencilled lettering: SOUTH EAST ANTRIM UDA

UFF and RATHCOOLE 1st BATTALION UDA-UFF

It faced a well-manicured roundabout in which the lampposts had been painted red, white, and blue, Loyalists flags fluttering in the breeze from the tops. There could be no doubt that this was a staunchly Loyalist area.

The Fern Lodge Bar & Grill on the Doagh Road in Rathcoole looked like a pink Toblerone. A mural for the 1st East Antrim UVF and East Belfast Young Citizens Volunteers adorned the wall and a spinning wind cock revolved on the roof of the building.

The YCV was formed in Belfast 1912. It was established to bridge the gap for eighteen- to twenty-five-year-olds between membership of youth organisations Boy Scouts and Boys' Brigade.

In the '70s this was usurped by the UVF to become a youth movement like the PIRA's Fianna Éireann and the Loyalist UDA's Ulster Young Militants, 'a military scouting movement which acted as a youth recruiting agency.'

He spotted the CCTV camera monitoring the entrance beside a sign which proclaimed that the bar was housed within the Wineway off licence.

Inside there were a wall of gaming machines and a pool table. Different sports channels were displayed on several large television monitors which fought for space on the walls between Manchester United, Liverpool and Rangers memorabilia. What walls you could see were painted in a lurid orange and blue.

You would never get that on the mainland, Johnno thought: United and Liverpool on the same wall. You wouldn't even get their mementos in the same pub.

A couple of surly youths were stood around the pool table, coins were lined along the wooden frame. A tall bald man with tattoos on his face and neck was looking for an angle to take a shot. They all went silent as he walked in.

The barmaid seemed cheerful enough. Bleached blonde hair, large false eyelashes. Her make-up was laid on thick above large red pouting enhanced lips.

"How about ya?" she asked, a twinkle in her eye, her leopard print blouse hardly concealing her large breasts. The size of her breasts was obviously helpful in keeping her upright as her backside was just as big, her tight black leggings showing that her G-string knickers were flossing her arse.

"Tennent's please, darling," he requested, not attempting to hide his accent.

In the mirror behind the bar, he watched the reaction from the pool table. They were huddled, possibly looking at a mobile phone, planning what to do next to the fly that had walked voluntarily in to the spider's web.

"Here's your pint, darlin'. Do ya wanna start a tab?" she asked, all smiles and tits.

The black leggings were two sizes too small for her ample legs. Her gold loop earrings bounced off her jowls as she spoke.

"I might just do that, my love. Now I've met you I might choose to stick around. I came in to meet an old army friend of mine, Dave Dove. Do you know him?"

The smile disappeared from her fat face; she became more concerned with cleaning the dirty glasses than the stranger.

"Dove? No, I've never heard of the guy," she lied.

Johnno ran the base of his pint glass along the bar top to ensure it slid smoothly along the freshly polished surface. He pulled a glass container with salted peanuts closer and again tested its ability to glide.

He looked up at the mirror to monitor the approaching bald man. The tattoo on his face was a tear drop. He had black tattoos on his neck and a red hand of Ulster on the back of his right hand.

"Are you leching at my sister's tits?" The voice was deep and menacing.

"I bet you look at them when you're in the bath together," Johnno said without looking around.

"What?" The bald man was confused.

"Is she a good kisser? I'd like to bet that your kids have six fingers."

"Get off that fucking stool, you English prick!" the guy boomed.

Johnno checked the mirror. The big guy's back up were giggling.

"Do you put that voice on for fun? I mean, do you really believe that it makes you sound like a hard man? *Get off that fucking stool, you English prick,*" he mocked in a deep voice whilst picking up a handful of peanuts.

He still hadn't faced the aggressor, he was just using the mirror's reflection to judge the distance and read the man's body language. The guy had adopted a boxer's stance, weight over his right knee, hands up guarding the sides of his face.

One of the younger males by the pool table must have sensed the coming danger and picked up a pool cue.

Johnno took a glance to his right, a dart board with three darts stuck in the bull was on the wall.

Johnno's hands were now in his pockets. Still facing the bar, he was in a passive position, non-threatening.

"Come on, boys, I was just having a laugh, just taking the piss. I know she's not your sister. Mother, maybe!"

He felt a cold drop of sweat slowly make its way down his spine. He concentrated, trying to slow down his breathing and heartbeat. Control his body, his emotions.

Things were going to get violent quickly. The military termed it as 'Going loud'. It was very apt.

'Shock and awe', 'Speed, aggression, surprise' were the mantras going through his head as he felt his body begin to relax and accept the inevitable.

"I'll tell you what, big fella, I'll give you to the count of three."

The big man laughed behind him.

"Three you say?" He turned round to acknowledge his back up by the pool table.

Johnno was working to the Jack Reacher rule book. If you give your opponent a three count, start the count on three.

"THREE!"

He whipped his hands out of his pocket and launched the peanuts at the boxer, quickly spinning off his bar stool and stamping down with all his might on the exposed kneecap, sending it backwards, snapping the anterior cruciate ligament and ripping both the medial and lateral ligaments.

The boxer howled like a banshee trying to grab his now-loose lower right leg.

Johnno wrapped his hand behind his pint and launched it towards the guys at the pool table. This was quickly followed by the bowl containing the remaining peanuts.

He danced towards the dart board and extracted, turned and launched the three missiles in one move towards the cowing pool players.

He then quickly closed the distance to the pool table, launching a chair towards the three recoiling lads.

He headbutted the first youth with all his might on the bridge of his nose. It immediately distorted. He kept up the momentum by grabbing the second one behind the head and smashing his face into the corner of the pool table with a sickening thud.

The kid with the pool cue was backed into a corner, shaking like a shitting dog, a dart flopped lazily from his cheek. The leader was hopping around screaming: one of his allies was laid out on the floor, nose flat and oozing blood, and his last mate was slumped over a table with a huge red gash along his forehead.

He tried to swing the cue but was confined by the corner. Johnno spun on his left foot and hit the pool cue man in the eye with his elbow smashing the socket. His head ricocheted into the wall, cracking his skull, and loosening the dart which fell to the floor.

He moved back to the hopping man and kicked him in the shin of his good leg, then gave him an upper cut for good measure.

His head snapped back as bottom and top jaws smashed into each other, breaking teeth, and bone.

The guy with the broken nose was pulled to his feet, then dumped on to a chair.

Johnno rifled through the man's pockets until he found his phone.

He placed the phone in the palm of his hand and wedged it under the injured man's broken nose. The pressure caused enough pain to get his attention.

"Who do you work for, lad?"

The young man was in no fit state to resist. He quickly divulged that he was a member of the local Young Citizens Volunteers. The older guy was a fully-fledged UVF member.

They had been warned off that an old soldier might be in the area. He showed him a picture on his phone. It was the selfie taken by Dove at the Rain Bar.

"Tell me about Mr Dove," Johnno demanded.

"No, I can't he'd – aww...!"

Johnno had grabbed the youth's broken nose and pulled it straight.

"Let me just remind you who you should be more afraid of at this present moment."

The youth's eyes were already beginning to swell, the bulges beneath were turning a deep purple colour.

"Now, you were going to tell me about Dave Dove."

He spilt his guts. Dove was a prime mover in the organisation. They called themselves a paramilitary unit, but they were more like a crime gang.

The young man had joined the YCV like kids on the mainland had joined the Boy Scouts. He had learned to throw bricks and keep lookout rather than tie knots or put-up tents.

He had been told to smash shop windows and intimidate people who owed Dove money. Some were on the dole and using food banks, but Dove always wanted his cash.

Some of his friends had been on driving jobs, picking up boxes from the border and delivering them to 'the pig sty' which was somewhere up in the hills.

In recent weeks they had been given more 'targets' to remove from Rathcoole. He had taken part in firebombing houses and shops all along the coast. He began to sob.

One of his friends had recent been found nailed to the floor of a derelict house and burnt to death, his partner was missing. They all believed that the soldier had done it, and they were scared.

"I didn't want to get into this, but once you're in it's impossible to get out. If you miss a meeting, you either pay up or take a beating. Please don't burn me."

"Leave the country, go to the mainland and start your life again," Johnno advised.

"It's not so simple, everything that goes through the port is reported back to the organisation. If I got on the ferry without permission, they'd have boys from Scotland waiting for me by the time I docked on the other side. That's how we knew you were back over here."

Johnno calmly walked over to the bar. The blonde barmaid stood speechless.

"Sorry about the mess, love. Tell Dove that Johnno sends his best wishes."

Monkscoole House, Rathcoole

Thomas Parker was sitting in the back of a police car, his head in his cuffed hands. The demolition had gone to plan, and the tower block dropped into the exact area he had planned.

Monkscoole House was now just dust and rubble. Two yellow JCB diggers and grabbers were motionless on the heap of debris. Tipper trucks lay idle, one was surrounded by police tape whilst officers swarmed over the open back.

It was only when one of the diggers was dropping part of a support beam when they spotted the leg. The site manager had immediately phoned the police. Now Parker was going to be asked questions about site security and where he had purchased the Enegel explosive.

Two of his idiot workforce had taken shelter in the flats due to a small summer shower. Neither of them heeded the warning siren or were noticed as being missing by the on-site foreman, another UVF employed numpty.

If he told the police he was doing the job for the organisation he would go to prison and his family would be dead. If he took the rap himself, the cops would still know the UVF were behind the scam and he would still go to prison, but they might, just might, let his family live.

The Knockagh Monument

It was approaching three thirty in the morning when they left the car and began the close target reconnaissance. The Knockagh Monument overlooked Carrickfergus to the south, and to the north the South Woodburn Reservoir.

He was still reflecting on what the boy with the broken nose had told him. It appeared that everything going through Larne was controlled by Loyalist paramilitaries. He wondered why Greg discredited the intelligence that the UVF were in charge.

The moon was reflected off the artificial lakes beside the woodland at the bottom of the hill. The monument was a war memorial erected in remembrance of the men from County Antrim who had died in the First World War. The site was over a thousand feet above sea level and the largest war memorial in Northern Ireland.

He waited by the one-hundred-and-ten-foot basalt obelisk which was a replica of the Wellington Monument in Phoenix Park, Dublin, although half the height.

He looked at the monument's inscription. It was adapted from the hymn "O Valiant Hearts" by John S. Arkwright. It read:

"NOBLY YOU FOUGHT, YOUR KNIGHTLY VIRTUE PROVED

YOUR MEMORY HALLOWED IN THE LAND YOU LOVED."

"Very poignant," she whispered.

Johnno tightened the straps of his daysack and started to walk down the hill, followed by Flusky.

She had tucked a one-to-one radio in the cargo pocket of her trousers.

It was a clear night and they quickly made good time to get down the hill and cross the main road before entering the sanctuary of the wood.

Johnno had set his compass and walked straight on to the firebreak which he estimated would take him to the South Woodman Reservoirs. The waters were still, dark, cold, and foreboding.

He started to close down the pace as he began to approach the piggery complex. They walked slowly for five minutes, then knelt and listened for two.

The piggery was on the left side of the gravel track, surrounded by a stone wall and the coniferous wood. The area was in darkness, the only sound and movement was from a restless pig.

An old van was on the yard, its tyres flat. Johnno took out his night vision monocular and slowly scanned each individual structure and building.

An old Nissan hut, its half-cylindrical skin of corrugated iron was full of holes and dilapidated, surrounded by overgrown brambles and nettles on one side of the yard.

The dirty concreate yard was full of oil drums, empty wooden boxes and smashed up pallets. A large well-fed rat scurried between the debris.

A concrete the pig sty was opposite the Nissan hut beside a large new metal cattle shed which was guarded by CCTV cameras high in the eaves.

A strange place to have such complex security, he thought, before moving into the shadows afforded by the rusting van.

He removed the laptop from his rucksack and began attaching small black boxes and antennas.

"What's that?" she asked.

"We need to disrupt the CCTV without the owners knowing we've done it. We can't use brute force, or we'll show out, so it's a case of softly, softly catch the monkey."

He was concentrating on the screen as it began to look for signals in the area.

"It should be easy enough. I doubt whether there'll be much activity from anywhere else. Bingo!" he announced.

He looked at the IP banner and then copied the details into the laptop's search engine. The Internet Protocol was a unique string of characters which identified each computer.

Within a minute he had identified the CCTV security system, the company which had set up the cameras and the default passwords and administration protocols to reset and override them.

"I thought it might take some time, but this hasn't been well protected. I've put my own default on the password so the cameras will send me any updates."

He started reviewing old footage. It was a busy place with men taking large packages out throughout the day. None looked like pig farmers.

"Whoever the owner is he mustn't trust his staff. It looks like he's been spying on his workers, he trusts no-one."

He then began tapping furiously on the keypad.

"What are you doing?" she whispered.

"I've replayed yesterday's recording as the live feed. Anyone who logs in thinking they're looking at what's happening at the site will actually be watching yesterday's feed. The weather was the same and I guess the light equally so."

The next obstacle was more substantial, a ten-lever Ingersoll lock. Johnno had used these devices before. In the military the ten-lever core was strong enough to protect weapons and ammunition stores. It was branded as a 'Miracle Lock.'

The lock was defending a thick metal door with solid iron hinges which were bolted into the frame.

Fortunately, Johnno had also come across this type of lock during his locksmith course.

He immediately got to work by using a heavy tension bar from his lock picking kit. He moved the bar to the optimal angle and using the pick he carefully felt for the ten clicks, five on either side.

He kept changing the tension tool's angles, muttering under his breath as he changed from one pick set to a spanner set.

The lock turned slightly with the spanner set using a rocking motion: he then changed back to use the tip of the rake pick to lift the pins to the shearline one at a time, feeling and hearing each click.

Whichever security company had sold the lock had changed the rubber O ring to dampen the clicks, giving Johnno less feedback to feel the pins' clicks as they became deactivated, making the whole process more difficult.

After fifteen minutes of sweating and mumbling he felt the core move the actuator which in turn released the locking ball bearings. It took one final click to make the cylinder turn and the plug rotate freely.

He made a mental note to be more 'creative' the next time he needed to defeat a lock.

Slowly he pulled open the door. It creaked and groaned.

"Wipe your feet," he whispered and slowly crept inside.

There was a small office on the right with a modest desk and the fittings for a laptop and internet access.

The second room was a storeroom. Shelves were stacked neatly with bottles of chemicals and boxes of powders. A central table was covered in a film of white dust. A digital set of scales was prominent on top.

"This is a mixing and cutting room, look at the air conditioning unit on the ceiling," he pointed out.

In a larger room there were more broken pallets. Johnno shone his head torch on the wood, carefully examining each piece.

"Look at the drilled holes in the larger parts of the pallets. They've been importing drugs in the wooden supports. Very clever, as customs would be looking at what's on the pallets, not the pallets themselves."

He remembered the pallets which were in the ISO container in which Ratty committed suicide at the Port of Salford. Perhaps that was the port of entry for the drugs.

Legitimate imports were taken from the pallets, one going for sale, the other being transported in bulk to Northern Ireland.

Another room had shelves bulging with prescription drugs and bags of white and brown powders. Heroin and cocaine, he suspected. These packages were different. Probably traded with another drugs gang as these baggies looked like they had already been cut and mixed.

They didn't need to look into the next room as the smell of cannabis hung in the air.

The final room was a brewery. Potatoes were in a large fermenting bin in one corner. A poteen still was in the corner and a hundred bottles filled with a clear liquid were on the shelves. A label with Mountain Tea was on each bottle.

"A tidy little business. Shall I give Greg a call?" Flusky asked.

He thought for a moment, then took out a small digital video camera and recorded everything they had found.

After checking that they had left no ground sign they left, ensuring that he turned over some pins on the Ingersoll lock. Whoever the key holder was they would think that the lock opened up a bit easier than usual. He would never know that only two pins were in place instead of the full ten.

A few of the pigs grunted as they passed. Flusky shone her torch inside the compound and stopped dead.

"Johnno, look at that."

He looked carefully at the spot in the pig shit she was indicating.

"Is that a bone?" he asked.

"No, to the left. Look, it's a wee finger."

He filmed the area then carefully picked up the tiny digit and placed it into a plastic bag.

They retraced their steps back to their parked car. Whilst Flusky poured out hot soup from a flask he called Greg.

He was surprised when the phone was answered immediately. A light sleeper, or was he on night duty?

"Are you working, mate?" he asked.

"No, er, just a difficult lambing. I'm with the, er, vet."

There was a pause.

"Sorry to bother you, mate, but I've just been talking to a guy in a bar who suggested that I look for a pig sty in some woods up in the Antrim hills. I know it's a long shot, but have you ever heard of anything like that?"

"Erm, no. The Antrim hills are a big place, and they have lots of woods and lots of pigs. I'll ask around when I get in work tomorrow. Who was the guy you were speaking to? Perhaps I could get more from him."

"Sorry, mate, he was in a bar on the Shankill, bit pissed to be honest. I'll do a Google recce in the morning." He clicked off the phone.

He took out his laptop and re-engaged the link with the CCTV cameras covering the piggery.

"What are you doing now?" she asked as she passed him a steaming cup of tomato soup.

"I'm going to catch a lying bastard. I am right in thinking that we are now in August?"

"Do I look like a friggin' calendar?"

"So how come lambs are being born in August when lambing season is March till May?"

It took ninety minutes till he saw the lights of the van arrive outside the piggery. The first rays of light were just creeping over the horizon.

He pressed 'record' as a half dozen men began moving everything from inside the building. A yellow JCB appeared trundling up the road.

The stillness of the morning was shattered by gunshots: roosting birds took flight, startled by the noise. The JCB disappeared towards the pig sty.

An hour later everything was empty, including the pig sty, which had been hosed down. It was clean enough for a royal inspection.

"I think we have a grass." he said as he closed down the laptop.

As the large white van left the dirt track and joined the tarmac road Dove called his boss.

"Yes, I know it's early, but I had a call from your brother-in-law this morning. We had a problem, now its verging on a fucking disaster."

There was shouting down the line.

"Listen, Bobby, the fucker is on to me. He went to the Fern and battered a few of the boys. Fucking idiots tried to take him on themselves and paid the price."

"He knows too much, he has to go," Charlton ordered.

CHAPTER TEN

Loughside, MI5 HQ, Belfast

Johnno had placed his laptop on the table and pressed 'play'. The computer was linked to a large overhead screen. Phos had invited a number of his colleagues to watch.

A plastic evidence bag rested beside the laptop.

"Did you have a surveillance authority for this?" someone at the back asked.

Johnno pointed at his wrist.

"Off the cuff, mate. I will of course be seeking an urgent oral authority immediately," he quipped quoting the official police directive.

There were a few laughs from the old operators and a few gasps from the new ones.

The first recording finished, then a second one took its place. The second video was done in broad daylight, showing the empty rooms, and cleared pig sty.

The camera focused on a small blood trail.

"What's that?" somebody asked.

"We heard gunshots when the clean-up party arrived, so we assume that they shot the pigs."

"Why shoot the pigs, did they think they were going to blab?"

"No, they probably thought they would shit out more evidence."

He picked up the evidence bag and threw it to the man who asked the question.

"Inside the bag is a child's finger, the rest of the hand was probably being digested inside one of those pigs."

There was an audible gasp from round the room.

"Pigs are a great way of disposing evidence. I suggest you start looking at the lists of missing children and check the DNA of that finger."

He then pressed 'play' on audio. The voices of Sir John Smythe and Robert Charlton were clear.

"I take it that your CHIS Charlton has not spoken about his relationship with his local MP or the reference to trafficking?"

The room was silent. A few of the assembled crowd looked at the walls, trying to avoid his eye contact.

"The problem that you're going to find with this case is an old one, which I did believe at one time had been eradicated, and that is collusion."

Fast Move, Templepatrick Road, Ballyclare

"Look, I can't stop the next shipment, it's almost across the border and will be here in the next few hours. I'll try to get them moved over to Scotland as quick as I can. The family have already got the other goods ready, and I have a van on the way to the pickup."

There was shouting on the other side of the phone.

"Look, they're lords, aristocracy. We can't just go over and waste the fuckin' lot of them. Yes, I know they're loose ends, but starting whacking senior judges and former members of parliament will attract more attention than if we waste this ex-squaddie that's bringing us all this grief. I'm trying to find the girl he's shacked up with. She's over in Bangor and I've got my best men on it."

He threw down the encrypted phone. 'King Billy' certainly had his knickers in a twist. He'd probably had a rollocking from Sir John and shit only flowed one way, downwards. He got back on the internet and started searching for Claire Flusk.

What he didn't realise was that at that precise moment she was sitting less than a mile away and knew full well where he was.

Kathmandu Inn, Indian & Nepalese food

They had driven past the Fast Move premises earlier in the morning. They had observed a line of white vans neatly arranged at the front of the low office block.

Pantech vans and flatbed lorries were arranged in different parking bays. The yard had an air of a well-run military organisation.

There was a larger garage behind the obligatory security fence line which had CCTV cameras on each corner covering the approaches and further cameras covering the yards and entrances to the main offices.

The yard was part of a big industrial estate which backed on to farm land. Claire and Johnno had already set up a base in a nearby derelict farm and inserted their own covert camera to monitor movement to and from the complex.

The night before they had used the Six Mile river to silently creep up to the fence and place the disguised camera.

Johnno again had tried to locate the server linked to the Fast Move security cameras but due to the number of businesses in the vicinity it was taking up valuable time.

He was just about to tuck in to his ordered Kathmandu chilli chicken when he dropped his fork.

"What a thick bastard."

He had been looking at his open laptop on the table as it continued to scroll through the possible servers.

"It was the same security firm that set up the piggery, same passwords, and security protocols. What a friggin' numpty," he rebuked himself.

"If you'd spend less time looking at my skinny arse and concentrate on your work, we'd get this job done," she teased.

They quickly finished their meals and drove back to the deserted farm. By the time they had arrived back Johnno was noting every camera location.

Fast Move, Templepatrick Road, Ballyclare

"Do you always move this quick?" she asked.

"I've got a fast arse, you know that." he said, never taking his eyes off the laptop screen.

"No operations. We're bouncing from one location to another without thinking."

"Following the intelligence, we do it quite a lot, risk assessments are made on the hop as more information is gathered and linked. The boys in the military did it all the time in Iraq and Afghanistan. Tiring, I know, but it gets results."

Two red ISO containers had arrived through the night and been unloaded at the rear of the office building. Johnno noted the identification numbers and passed them to Flusky.

"Phone DCI Wood in Manchester and ask her if she can spare one of her team to see if these ISO's have come from the Port of Salford." He asked throwing her his phone.

The feed from the covert micro camera showed the arrival of a car bearing Southern Irish number plates.

A tall man wearing a blue baseball cap got out of the driver's door and helped a young boy of about seven years old from the back passenger seats. He was in and out of the office in less than five minutes.

A second car from the Republic soon arrived, this time driven by an overweight woman. She took a small boy from the rear of the vehicle and quickly departed.

"Is this a crèche?" Johnno commented.

He picked up his phone and hit the number for 'Ma.'

The call was quickly answered.

"Look, Ma, I think I do need your help. I'm watching a place and two cars from the Republic have just dropped off children. I can't trust the cops to do anything without getting compromised." He relayed the registration numbers of each vehicle.

"Thanks for the call and you're right not to trust anybody. Some of my men arrested a fella trying to burn Nationalist families out of their homes in Antrim the other day. He's told us that Charlton and Dove are trying to get the Peelers very busy looking at sectarian violence while they run drugs up from the south and bring in millions of illegal ciggies." The line went dead.

His worst fears were confirmed that the Republicans were now in the game and looking to retaliate against the growing attacks against Catholics. God help the 'arrested fella', Johnno thought.

He had gained control of the outside CCTV cameras which overlooked the yard and lines of parked vehicles.

The system showed the same similarities to the one at the piggery, but no cameras inside. He began to connect more small black boxes to his laptop.

"What are those things?" she asked nonchalantly.

He continued setting up the hacking tools. He pointed to the first box.

"This is SHODAN a specialised search engine. It finds IP banners and tells you what's behind the IP address, and this little beauty is a Hacks Cloud Command & Conquer. It forces all devices to link to my laptop so I can then remotely access their systems."

The locations of the cameras were not ideal. One just looked towards the entrance door, a second faced the back door and the third faced a green door somewhere inside the office building.

"Eureka!" He shouted as he finally connected with the cameras inside the Fast Move offices. The picture quality was poor and grainy but was good enough to identify people's faces.

The yard was busy, trucks, vans and Pantechs coming and going all through the day. Men carrying bunches of keys left without them.

Then a man arrived carrying a cardboard box. It was late in the afternoon, too late for dinner, they both thought. The guy disappeared to a waiting van, counting some cash.

It was only then that he saw the small man. He wore a black baseball cap and was carrying the cardboard box. He took an age to unlock the green the door.

Inside the door was a cage, four young boys were sleeping on a dirty mattress on the floor. They resembled miniature blanket men, from the old IRA protests in the Maze prison.

The small man shoved the box into the cage and quickly locked the green door. He briefly looked up towards the camera. Dove, without question.

"Quick, get on to your Crimestoppers or any mates that are willing to do you a favour and call this in."

She made the call immediately.

Johnno was surprised when his phone rang next.

"Greg," he whispered before he answered.

"Hi, mate, how can I help you?"

"Some stuff came in about the Watson case. Any chance you can meet me up in Larne and discuss it?" he asked.

"Yeah, I'll give you a bell back once I've checked my diary. I'm over in Portadown at the moment." He lied.

He took the sim card out of the device and put the phone down, then began loading everything back into his rucksack.

"Let's move," he shouted across to Flusky.

"What's going on?"

He looked at the laptop. He wasn't the only one on the move. The green door was open and the cage empty. He looked at the other CCTV feeds. The kids were being loaded into the back of a van. A second van was being loaded with boxes.

"I think that our friend Greg has been watching all of the incidents on your intelligence system. He's picked up on your call and warned off Dove. I'd also bet that he's trying to get a GPS signal for my phone, so we need to move."

HMP Long Lartin

The curry pot noodle wasn't being eaten because he was hungry, but because he was bored. Another day looking at a tiny TV. He didn't play on the Xbox like his cellmate who was much younger.

Alan Sampey looked over his shoulder towards the door. Another prisoner stood there looking at him.

"Terry, fancy a game of pool?" he asked the long-haired youth busy working his way through the next level of his game.

"Nah, I'm trying to get this finished." He was trying his best to concentrate.

"Yes, you fuckin' do. Come with me, you fuckin' bell-end." He was insistent.

Terry looked across to the door then, as if a bomb had gone off, threw the game controls on his bed and jumped off the top bunk making his way out of the cell, muttering as he left.

A cartoon car was on the screen being passed by other cartoon vehicles. Sampey noticed that the visitor had left a mop and bucket at the cell door.

Johnno's warning immediately came to mind. A cold sweat ran down his back. He looked for a weapon. The kettle was empty of boiling water. The fork he was holding was plastic.

Two prisoners appeared at the door, looking either way to check for any guards. A third prisoner moved quickly between them. He wore only a pair of shorts; his black skin shone after being shaved of any body hair and lathered up with soap so any blood could be quickly washed off.

"Bobby says hello, you fuckin' grass!" he whispered as he lunged at Sampey.

His hands were huge and almost covered his victim's skull. Sampey tried to escape by pushing himself back under his mate's bunk.

The assailant's grip on his head was making him grow dizzy as he dragged him back from the shadow of the bunk bed into the light. His neck was being arched and it felt like it was going to break.

In his other hand the attacker held an orange piece of plastic from a broken disposable razor. The blade has been broken off then melted into the handle by the side of a second blade a millimetre to its side to make an improvised double-edged knife.

Four slices are all it took to sever the arteries. Less than two minute later Sampey would be dead. No loose ends.

One of the guys standing guard picked up the mop bucket and threw it over the attacker. Blood rushed off his skin.

Marcel leaned over to the small toilet in the corner and dropped the improvised knife in the bowl before flushing the evidence away.

He marched out of the cell and into the showers. One of his gang handed him a phone, it was tiny, a Zanco. An Irish voice on the other end of the line said "Hello".

"It's done, Bro!" he said and handed the phone back to his runner who quickly plugged the phone up his arse.

Marcel Skillen, a lifer, top jockey in the Birmingham Crew, incarcerated - but fifty grand richer.

CHAPTER ELEVEN

Fast Move, Templepatrick Road, Ballyclare

Dove slammed the phone down. Behind him one of the children was still crying after being scolded by one of his henchmen.

"Dembo, shut that little fucker up and then round up the boys! We need to move all the gear. It looks like we've been blown. Get a few vans ready!" he screamed.

Four men approached from the rest room and grabbed keys from the wall and began preparing escape vehicles.

Antrim Coast Road

Claire starred at him in amazement. Her mobile had been emitting a 'Star Wars' theme which usually heralded the arrival of Darth Vader.

"Hello, Ma'am, can I help you?"

He could hear the muttering on the other end of the line.

"But I'm on leave, Ma'am," she tried to explain before the phone went dead.

He took a quick glance at her; she was ashen and shaking.

"Anything I need to know?" he asked.

"That was Superintendent Hayley Canning of C Branch Specialist Operations. Apparently, she's now my boss and she wants me to report to her immediately at the Knock."

She went on to explain that Canning was a late entry graduate officer who had been placed on the rapid promotion scheme. After gaining rave reviews for reorganising PSNI's administration unit she had requested and been given a move to the Crime Division.

In a short space of time, she had made her mark by insisting that surveillance officers drive round in pairs to save on fuel and cars, cutting overtime to a minimum and moving any experienced officer who challenged her accountant's approach to covert policing.

She was known as a bean counter; she questioned any requisition for new equipment and refused to sign off any speeding or parking tickets accrued by the teams.

There were tears in her eyes.

"What's going on, Claire?"

"She's threatened to sack me for working on an unsanctioned job. I have to go and see her immediately, not even go home and get changed."

Johnno pulled the car over.

"How does she know you're not at home? Just wait a minute, let me sort this out."

He grabbed his phone and replaced the sim card, whilst walking away from the car. She watched him pace up and down, gesticulating with his free arm every now and again.

He returned and threw the phone down into the console. He spun the car and headed off towards Belfast.

"Are you taking me to the Knock?"

"No, we're going to Palace Barracks. I smell a rat. Did she ever work with Greg Tams?"

Alina Road, South Armagh

The cartel was taking extra caution on the shipment since the news of the problems emanating up in Belfast.

Two motorcycle outriders drove on ahead to clear the route and warn of any Garda activity. They used only small unlit roads as they approached the border.

The meeting place was a derelict barn which straggled the border on the Alina Road in South Armagh. It was a moonless night, either side of the road were high banks with blackthorn bushes on top.

The time and place of the handover had been divulged by a naked man hung upside down in a barn after being captured by a Republican snatch team. Beside him was a naked woman captured as she travelled back South after dropping off a child at the van hire centre.

Both were now dead and the death warrants on the drug dealers and child abductors they worked for signed. Kate Fitzpatrick had already instructed Sean McGivern, the head of Republican intelligence, to prepare the shadow group Direct Action Against Drugs for a major operation on both sides of the border.

The taller bike rider was lucky as the taut metal wire which was strung across the road cut through his biceps before flinging him off his bike. The smaller rider wasn't so lucky and was instantly decapitated.

The following black BMW only briefly caught the advanced guard in their headlights before the shooting started.

A heavy machine gun opened up, ripping the bodywork of the vehicle to pieces. The car veered into the bank as a burst of bullets hit the driver in his chest and head.

The vehicle flipped, then slid down the road on its roof until coming to a spinning stop just yards from the border.

Immediately two cars darted away from their hiding place in the old barn quickly heading into the darkness of the North.

The ambush team checked the bodies and administered a coup de grâce to the car party. The armless man lay in the middle of the road, whimpering.

"Tell your masters that we'll be coming for them if they don't stop their anti-social behaviour in twenty-four hours. They'll face the wrath of Direct Action Against Drugs. You have been warned."

One of the volunteers phoned the Garda whilst the leader phoned an old woman in Belfast.

"Ma! It's done."

"Well done! Our organisation is about to mount the night of the long knives in Dublin and Drogheda. We are going to reclaim the streets," the woman said before putting down the encrypted phone.

Palace Barracks

Phos had a beaming smile when he re-entered the office.

"A good job you had the sense to call in, Johnno. A Det surveillance team has just identified a hit squad on the route you would have taken to your meeting with Ms Canning. I've got Counter Corruption inbound to secure her and any communications devices. Once she's in the pen we'll hit the team on the ground. Looks like you've been upsetting somebody, Phillip!"

"Who the hell has managed to get at a high-ranking police officer? Claire has described her as a flyer. Why would she jeopardise everything to be involved in a murder?"

"Powerful people who can offer her another step up the promotion ladder. You might like to know that her father is a close friend of Sir John Smythe."

"What about Tams?"

"Your suspicions were correct. He's served with Canning and apparently, he's somewhere along the coast carrying out his duties as the small ports officer."

"What a load of bollocks," Johnno exclaimed.

"He has access to every jetty and airfield on his patch. For all we know he might be organising his escape. Even Hendo can't get a location for his mobile. It looks like he's gone to ground and ditched the phones we know he has."

They looked out of the window towards the halogen security lights which ringed the fence, turning night into day.

Phos put his hand on his former Sergeant's shoulder.

"You've got them running scared Johnno, now go out and finish the job."

Salt Mines, Carrickfergus

Dove was sweating. He had just carried the last container into the deep storage facility. The metal shelves were stacked with boxes of cigarettes, drugs, and bundles of cash.

The cash had been neatly arranged into Dollar, Euro, and Pound notes.

Greg Tams had just left with a wad of Euros which he was hoping would take him far away. Dove had been contemplating whacking him and dumping his carcass out at sea, but he had the feeling that Tams had taken out protective measures by making records of his involvement.

It was a good idea, something which he himself had already done.

He took a quick snort from an open bag of white powder, each of his men also took a nose full.

It had been a quick dash from the vehicle depot: one of the men had taken a vehicle away to hide the children and the rest rushed to the deep tunnel hived off the main driveway into the salt mine.

As the tunnels became deeper the management came up with the profitable idea that the unused portion of the site could be used to store delicate items.

There was practically no humidity at that depth so documents could be safely stored. Banks, large corporations and even PSNI had their own private vaults.

 The cannabis bundles had been moved to another hide location as the sweet-smelling aroma would have hung in the still air of the tunnel.

Torbergel Lane, Larne

There were rolling green fields as far as the eye could see. Sheltered in a small valley was the farm house miles away from anywhere.

Claire had made a few calls whilst Johnno was talking to Phos and finally found Greg's home address. The property was far from being a smallholding as he'd described it.

The farmhouse was large and modern, there were three huge cattle sheds which appeared to have been recently built. The gardens, fields and hedgerows were all well maintained.

There were no signs of sheep in any of the surrounding pastures, in fact no animals at all apart from the distant barking of a dog.

"How much do PSNI cops get paid over here?" he asked.

She was already shaking her head. "Not enough to own or maintain that place."

Claire had tucked their car into a field and was trying to observe any movement towards Tam's home.

It was another baking hot day; they had the windows open and sat in silence, apart from the occasional buzz from a bee looking for pollen.

"Greg came to my brother's funeral. He said he was a friend of Derek's," She was speaking out loud, voicing her deepest thoughts.

He could feel her anger grow.

"We don't know anything yet, Flusky, it's just a bunch of coincidences. A great man once said, 'A riddle, wrapped in a mystery, inside an enigma'."

A heat haze was raising from the fields, making it difficult to see clearly. She held the binoculars up to her eyes which made her perspire even more.

They couldn't run the car's engine so there was no air conditioning. They both sat in their leather seats and continued to sweat.

"Stand By, Stand By, movement," she whispered.

Four large box-bodied vans in convoy turned off the main road and headed down the path towards Tam's farm complex.

A woman met them at the end of the drive and pointed to one of the barns. Each carefully reversed into the gaping doorway and disappeared inside.

Pamela Tams was flustered. The call she had taken from her brother had insisted that he needed help fast, and he had reminded her in no uncertain terms that she had a debt to settle.

There was a strong sweet smell as the men from the vans hurriedly moved a multitude of bags from the vans to a corner of the barn.

"Any chance of a cuppa, Missus?" one of the guys asked.

She looked at him over her expensive thick black rimmed glasses.

"Just dump your stuff and get off my property," she scolded him.

He snatched her by the back of her head, turning it to face him. He was close enough that spittle landed on her face as he talked.

"Your fuckin' brother's property, and he's the only reason I've not slapped you then bent you over and fucked you. Now go and get the kettle on before I let my dick rule my head."

He pushed her to her knees and rubbed her face into his crotch. He was laughing, his friends standing behind him were also chuckling.

She realised that her brother was in serious trouble; he was weak and vulnerable. His protection wouldn't help her or Greg any more. She hurried away, tears in her eyes.

Flusky relayed the events to Johnno who pushed his head back into the headrest.

"Call it in right away, I'm going to try and call Greg."

They both reached for their mobiles.

He was shocked that Greg picked up his call after the first ring. He knew that Hendo would also be tracking the movement of Greg's handset. He wondered how he had kept the phone concealed from Hendo over that last few hours.

"Hi, Greg, it's Johnno. I won't keep you on long as you're going to get a call from your wife. It appears that you're in a world of shit, my friend. You'd better get home right now." He threw the phone down.

Claire was just giving the operator the location of the farm before ringing off.

"At least he won't be able to check our location on any computer if he's rushing to get home," Johnno chuckled.

The police car arrived just in time to stop Greg using his issued police pistol shooting the guy that had grabbed Pam. In the distance Johnno and Claire could hear sirens as the back-up team arrived.

Johnno switched on the car radio and placed on his sunglasses. The Style Council was blasting out: "Walls come tumbling down."

"How very apt," Claire giggled.

The song stopped as a newsreader interrupted the broadcast for an immediate newsflash. The mutilated bodies of four young boys had been found on Larne Road by a dog walker.

"I think it's time to speak to the Boss," Johnno commented as they moved out of the field and back on to the road.

Seskin Road, Straid, Co Antrim

Johnno checked the moving icon on his laptop and estimated that they would arrive at the mansion right behind Sir John.

Claire stopped the car at the black ornate iron gates to allow Phil to open them. 'Ponderosa' had been painstakingly welded into the design and painted gold.

As Claire drove on to the gravel drive, he did a cursory search of the landscape. The lawns were neatly trimmed and smelled like they had recently been mown.

Beyond the road was a field of cows penned in by thick black bush hedges. The field gently rose to the south west. At the top of the hill was a small copse of trees. He saw a red vehicle, possibly a pick-up truck, parked to the side, silhouetted on the skyline. Something glinted in the hedge line as an object reflected the sunlight.

'absence of the normal, presence of the abnormal.'

He returned to the vehicle and grabbed something from the boot before getting back into the car. He leaned over to kiss her cheek and took the chance to whisper in her ear. He threw something on her lap as he left.

She pulled up the car behind Sir John's. The great man was admiring a very colourful rose bed. He was in shirt sleeves, his tie knot loose.

He looked towards the new arrival. Only Johnston exited the vehicle.

"Can I help you?" he asked.

"Sir John, I think you want to speak to me, so here I am."

The older man stared in anger.

"Who are you? This is private property; I'll have you know."

"I think you know very well who I am, but what you think I've done is a complete lie."

He moved towards the MP and positioned himself with his back to the rose bushes. Sir John moved to his left to stand directly in front of the usurper.

"I believe that you were told that I was involved in the murder of your son during a military operation in Belfast." Johnno spoke slowly, deliberately.

Smythe was clenching his teeth as if he was going to listen to a revelation that he did not want to hear.

"Davie Smythe was given a warning, and in my opinion was going to surrender as he was surrounded by soldiers."

"So why did you bastards gun him down?" Smythe's face was reddening, the veins in his neck bulging.

Johnno noticed the glint of sunlight on the hill again and took a step closer to Sir John.

"Your son was shot by one of his comrades who was running from the scene, someone that I believe you know: Robert Charlton."

"Rubbish. Charlton is a fine man! He was lucky to escape with his life. He told me that you fuckers executed my boy. Robert was shot whilst escaping."

"Charlton was given the wound so nobody would think that he was an informer. He continues to work for the security forces. He's fed you a lie to ingratiate himself to you, but then again, I think he's also providing an even worse service for you. Tell me about the children," he demanded.

The conversation was interrupted by Sir John's phone beeping. He looked at the screen. The name shown was 'King Billy'.

Johnno recognised the EncroChat phone. He again questioned himself as to why an MP would need such a clandestine device.

It was instinct: a millisecond of an orange flash from the copse that made him turn. The bullet slammed in between Smythe's shoulder blades, tearing his heart and lungs in the process. The round then exited his breast bone and hit the turning Johnston in the rib cage.

The kinetic energy hit him like a mule kick. He felt his ribs crack as he spun round landing face-first into the roses. The thorns tore at his exposed face.

Warm, wet, sticky blood covered him.

Nothing moved, Claire was nowhere to be seen. A long minute passed, then a vehicle could be heard moving down from the hill. The red pick-up drove back towards the coast.

Claire heard the vehicle's engine slowly disappear into the distance before she ran towards the scene.

Sir John lay face down on the driveway, his white shirt covered in dark red blood. He wasn't moving, and never would again.

"Did you ring the cops?" Johnno groaned.

She lifted him slowly. He yelped as the thorns scratched him again. He blinked and tried to wipe Sir John's blood off his face.

"How did you know?" she asked.

"I trained the little Brummie bastard. Fortunately, he forgot to cover up the lens of his telescope when looking towards the sun. I think I caught him out a few times during his sniper badge tests for the same thing."

He had scratches on his face and hands, his polo shirt was splattered with blood, but luckily none of it was his.

"Are you sure you're, OK?" she asked.

He gingerly removed his shirt to reveal a strange-looking vest. It looked like it had scales.

"Something I was given when I worked with the Americans in Fort Bragg. It was an experimental body armour called Dragon's Skin."

Pinnacle Armor, an American company, had designed a radical new type of protective armour which was both lightweight and small enough to wear under everyday clothing. It could absorb a high number of bullets because of its unique design, involving circular discs that overlapped each other.

The company had developed the design after studying ancient Chinese armour which used bound clumps of hay.

The American Special Forces had been given a job lot to trial and evaluate, which is how it had made its way into Johnno's stash.

Apart from a cracked rib or two he was fine.

"Thank god I decided not to hand this body armour back in!" he exclaimed.

"We'd better get a move on; the cops are on the way, and we need to find a red pick-up truck," she reminded him as she knelt to pick up Sir John's phone.

He grabbed a new T shirt. A large purple bruise was already forming over his ribs, and it hurt like hell. He grabbed some painkillers from his bag and a bottle of water.

Claire checked the battery life of the deceased man's phone then placed it into a Fereday evidence bag.

"Dove probably thinks I'm dead or he would have put another round in me while I was down. Big mistake, Dovey. Big mistake."

She wheel spun the car off the drive and began the pursuit.

CHAPTER TWELVE

Salt Mine, Carrickfergus

Dove had managed to get back to the new hide in the salt mine without any trouble. He had sent his men home, deciding on laying low in the shelter of the deep shaft.

His plan was to do some stocktaking by loading the money and cocaine on to a vehicle, then driving round to Charlton's house and shooting him in the face. He had enough contacts on the mainland to sell the gear and with the profit he would move far away.

He was on his second line of coke and feeling good. He felt a sense of pride in killing his teacher. All those times he had to do push-ups for committing a small misdemeanour or wear the pink-painted 'Dill of the Day' battle helmet for the biggest fuck up of the day.

Johnno was annoying because he didn't give the trainee snipers a bollocking: he was worse - he would take the piss mercilessly. He was funny and well-practised, so the other troops also joined in the ridiculing.

Dove hated it, nobody took the piss out of Dave Dove.

"Not so good at spotting now, are you, Johnno?" he shouted manically to no one in particular.

In the distance he heard vehicles and diggers moving down the main shaft towards the salt face and the main excavation work. He rolled out a sleeping bag and fell asleep.

Johnno finished off the bag of chips and threw the newspaper wrapper in the back.

They had easily caught up with the distinctive red pick-up and trailed it from a distance to the area of the salt mines.

Content that Dove had driven his vehicle into the entrance they sat back and waited for darkness before making their approach.

The pawns had slowly been removed from the table, now it was time for the major pieces to be taken before the final check mate.

Johnno had busied himself checking the internet about the layout of the mine and had even found a map of what lay behind the large green door.

Over to his left a red and black bulk container was at anchor. A yellow crane was busy bucketing in salt from the mines. There was an orange and pink dust falling from each movement of the machinery.

There was a small portacabin which he assumed the Ports Officer, Greg Tams, would have used to inspect incoming and outgoing cargo.

It all made sense now, the links to the Port of Salford, the ability to move drugs, guns, and people under the watchful eye of a friendly PSNI officer.

Hendo's inability to trace Tam's mobile was probably due to him having the device with him whilst being deep underground.

Claire wasn't very talkative, unlike Greg Tams. He had been arrested at his farm and almost immediately began spilling the beans. He had kept records, lots of them backed up with taped conversations between Charlton and Dove.

One of his revelations had been that he had been with Claire's brother when he was murdered by Dave Dove. His claim that he was too scared to report the incident due to being under threat from the UVF was bullshit.

"Don't worry, they'll unravel his story. Tams and his wife are going down for a long time. We now have to sort this little shit out."

"Are we planning to arrest him?" she asked.

"Hard arrest," he declared.

She looked at him puzzled. "What's a hard arrest?"

"Well, my love, we'll let Mr Dove decide how he wants to be arrested, with cuffs on or in a body bag. I think I know which he'll choose."

The entrance to the mine was via a large green dome shaped shed which led to a dual carriageway road a thousand meters underground.

The mine was almost sixty years old and had been considerably refined and developed over that time.

The number one shaft headed inland on a northerly direction for around five hundred metres on a one in five gradient. Rock salt pillars and conventional metal columns were set at intervals to hold up the roof.

Orange lighting illuminated the road. Off to the left and right were further smaller tunnels which had been added quite recently.

The main road was a dual carriageway, vehicles with orange flashing lights appeared to be leaving en masse as a siren began to wail.

The siren suddenly stopped, then the ground shook like an earthquake. A thin film of dust appeared from the darkness of the lower shaft. There was a smell of ammonia in the air.

A few minutes later a different siren and the vehicles started moving back towards the blasted rock salt.

Dumper trucks appeared from down the shaft, carrying large rocks into a shaft off to the left. A few moments later a crushing and popping noise began.

She touched his shoulder and pointed over to the left side of the road.

A red pick-up truck was parked and unattended on the right-hand side of the road. The shaft beyond was about ten metres high and fifteen metres wide.

The shaft to the right of the pick-up had a large sign: 'PSNI'. It had large steel gates and further thick oak doors on the inside.

The gate by the pick-up was made from thick galvanised steel, a heavy chain hung loose between each side. The shiny silver lock was an Ingersoll and took Johnno less than a minute to open.

There was an aperture in the fence which could enable somebody on the inside to lock and unlock the heavy Ingersoll device.

Cautiously they both walked down the black tunnel. They were split on either side of the shaft to prevent them being silhouetted against the bright tunnel they had left behind.

Little alcoves had been dug out on each side of the shaft. They stopped at each and checked the opening. Only once they were satisfied that nobody lay in wait did they switch on their small pen lights.

There were shelves of brown and white powders, boxes of pills and crystal-like rocks. He opened one of the many sports bags. It was full of cash.

Some of the pills had a Dove sign embossed on them. "Nothing like glorifying yourself," Claire whispered.

There was a large open bag of white powder by the entrance of another alcove beside some scales, vacuum packing, and money counting machines.

Johnno began to recognise some of the bags and equipment from the piggery. There were reams of cigarette packs: cigarettes from China. Counterfeit booze with new labels and designer clothing which was also probably fake.

They both heard it at the same time, a loud fart. She looked at him and giggled.

"The fart which got you killed," she whispered.

They switched off their pen lights and waited until their eyes had become accustomed to the darkness again.

Slowly they started to inch along the shaft until they reached the end wall. The shaft was now in a T shape with two sub-shafts on either side.

Johnno felt around the left side and touched the cold metal of a shelf. On the shelf was the familiar shape of an automatic pistol, beside it a submachine gun, probably a Scorpion.

He decided not to pick up either. In the darkness he couldn't tell just what state they were in and to see if either was loaded would have been noisy.

A groan and a shuffle, material rubbing on the floor. A nervous wait. Was Dove laying prone on the ground, gun in hand waiting? Then the grunt of a snore.

He inched forward agonizingly slowly, feeling his way with his feet. Bingo! He touched something soft; he could hear the man breathing by his left boot.

He flicked on his pen torch. Dove was wrapped up tight in a thick green army sleeping bag. His head was back in the hood, cutting off any chance of hearing any approach.

The draw cord which could tighten the hood lay loose. Johnno grabbed it and pulled it up tight before smashing a fist into the sleeping man's face.

"Early call, Dove," he shouted and started to drag the hapless man out of the shaft by the sleeping bag cord.

The whole room was then illuminated as Claire hit the light switch. They both blinked at the brightness.

There was a ripping sound as the large Bowie-shaped blade of a K Bar survival knife appeared in the middle of the green material and Dove rolled out on to the dusty floor.

Johnno gathered the ripped sleeping bag and threw it towards his knife wielding adversary.

The shiny blade flashed backwards and forwards. Dove was like a cornered rat.

"Stand down, Dove, it's over," Johnno ordered.

"Go fuck yourself, Sarge! I'm going to kill you like I did to your bird's brother, then I'll fuck her.

"Not with that little pecker of yours, it wouldn't touch the side, pencil dick."

Dove gave a guttural roar like a wounded animal and slashed out.

"Your gang in East Belfast are all about to be arrested or stood down permanently. Put the knife down or I'll ram it up your arse - and you know I can and will do it."

Dove had often been the 'Guinea Pig' when Johnno showed the troops unarmed combat techniques, but this time the knife he held was real, not made of rubber or a stick.

"Why did you get involved in all this shit? You were a British soldier, we don't take sides, we don't judge."

"I have my reasons."

"What, a reason that's worth dying for?"

They both spotted it at the same time, on a low shelf, a Browning Hi Power pistol.

Dove threw the knife towards his adversary and snatched up the gun. He pointed it gleefully but was surprised that Johnno was laughing.

"Is that the pistol you stole from the armoury in Ballykinler?" he asked.

Dove also laughed. "Yes, it is. It's got more notches than Clint Eastwood's bedpost. It's the gun I used to shoot her brother in the face - which is what I'm going to do to you."

Johnno whistled out. "Looks like you're learning your lesson, seeing that my body armour stopped the shot from your rifle. But you'd better come closer - or are you afraid, you little Brummie shit?"

Dove's hands were shaking. He held the pistol in one hand, arm fully stretched, then took a step forward.

Johnno was still smiling.

"What the fook are you laughing at?"

"You're a fuckin' bell-end Dove. Do you think for one moment that I would leave a loaded pistol next to you? Claire unloaded it before I woke you up. Now she has her personal protection weapon pointing at you and you have a gun in your hands. Self-defence, the coroner will say."

Dove turned the pistol in his hand, unsure, his cockiness gone, then looked into the shadows to look for the woman.

His hands trembled more, sweat ran down his forehead and stung his eyes. He needed another snort of the white powder as his head started to ache.

Johnno stepped forward putting his left-hand index finger in to the trigger guard and shoving back the top slide of the pistol with his thumb, pushing it back a few millimetres.

The movement was enough to activate one of the pistol's safety features and stop the weapon firing. He then pushed his right thumb into Dove's eye socket.

Dove lost all thought about the weapon and dropped it as his eyeball was pushed back towards his brain.

"Move, Johnno," he heard her scream.

Instinctively he released his grip and stepped left as two shots whizzed past his right shoulder. The first shot hit Dove in the throat, snapping his head back, quickly followed by the second which hit him beneath his chin and exited through the top of his head.

He turned and walked into the darkness. She was shaking, the gun still held outstretched in her long thin arms.

"What have I told you about playing with guns?"

He took it from her and unloaded the magazine, expertly catching the round as it ejected from the chamber.

"I didn't know you had put your body armour back on or unloaded his pistol?"

"I hadn't, I just needed to distract him long enough to get a little closer." He grinned.

His remark seemed to break the tension and she also smiled faintly.

"Get all the lights on and let's see what we've got. Come on, switch on, you're back in the game now - unlike the unfortunate Mr Dove." He kissed her forehead.

Dove had packed two large rucksacks with money, on top of one was an EncroChat phone. He checked the battery life which was low. He found the charging lead in one of the rucksack's pouches.

He left the phone in a Faraday bag to prevent any outside tampering whilst it fully recharged.

They placed the two rucksacks and three carrier bags of cash in the back of the red pick-up, then returned for the body.

Flusky's gun was still on the shelf.

"Hey, don't forget your pistol," he reminded her.

"That's not my pistol, I just took it off that shelf," she explained.

He took a step back in amazement.

"So how did you know it was loaded or even ready to fire?"

"I didn't."

He shook his head. "The luck of the Irish," he muttered.

They wiped down the pistol Claire had used to shoot Dove and recovered the empty shell case.

After rapping the remnants of Dove's head in a plastic bag they dragged his lifeless body along the shaft to the gate. A small trail of blood marked their route. A large yellow dumper truck sat idle in the middle of the main tunnel, which gave Johnno a brainwave.

He climbed up on to one of the large wheels then reached down and grabbed the dead man's hand from his partner. He heaved and grunted as he manoeuvred the body into place. Luckily the dump truck's tyres were wide and gave him an area to rest Dove's body before finally hoisting him into the bucket of the machine.

He jumped down beside her, his shirt damp with sweat and blood droplets.

"You need to get changed," she commented.

He ushered her towards the pick-up, and they immediately left the mine, leaving Dove's body to be covered in the next excavation of rocks, then dumped into the Stamler crushing machine.

The colossal machine was a drum feeder breaker with carbide-tipped picks, which broke the rock salt down to two hundred and fifty-millimetre blocks before being transported up one kilometre of conveyor to the main processing plant, which was a triple drum crusher.

It was just approaching dawn when they exited the mine. They had just loaded the last of the cash bags from the pick-up into Johnno's car when they heard the ring tone.

Dove's phone had fallen out of the Faraday bag, but again luck was on their side. The screen was illuminated with the name 'King Billy'.

"Mr Charlton, I presume, or should I call you the Gimp with a Limp?"

"Who the fuck is this?"

"I'm the man you were trying to kill. Now I'm putting an end to your little game once and for all."

He switched the phone off and sealed it inside the bag. He knew that the details on the phone along from with the one they had recovered from Sir John would be vital to any future investigation.

He took out his own mobile phone and made his own call.

"Phos, I need a favour, phone location and current vehicle for Charlton. You need to send a team to the salt mines over in Antrim. There's an Aladdin's cave of UVF goodies."

CHAPTER THIRTEEN

Beltoy Court, Carrickfergus

Charlton paced up and down the living room floor of his mistress's bungalow. His stocking feet sunk into to the white deep pile carpet.

He tried another number, again no reply. He was anxious as he couldn't raise any of his men and the Englishman had stolen Dove's phone.

He was so nervous that he broke protocol and used his personal Galaxy phone.

Dove never let him down, he'd do anything to please, no matter how heinous. Rape, torture, murder - he had no problems with. It was Dove's idea to dispose of the used kids by feeding them to the pigs.

He was a sick fuck but very useful. Now he had disappeared just when Charlton needed his expertise the most.

During his last call he had been bragging that he had killed Smythe and the Englishman with one shot. He'd seen confirmation on the news that the politician was dead, but no word about a second body.

His Galaxy phone vibrated in his hand, an unknown number. He hit the green button and listened.

"Is that Bobby the fuckin' grass?" A woman's voice. She sounded angry.

"Who is this?"

"Are you still bucking that whore Cilia on the Beltoy estate, Bobby? Cos we're coming to give you the eight ball." The phone went dead.

The legendary 'eight ball' punishment was the ultimate penalty. Few survived being shot in each ankle, knee, elbow, and wrist - and those that did wished they didn't.

His nearest safe house was along the coast in a small village in Whitehead. He had friends in the village, a stash of money and a spare passport. There was also a pistol and an AK47 to defend himself.

At last, he had a positive idea: his handler in MI5. She could be his guardian angel. He scrolled down until he found the number.

She was a great woman, pretty too, always answered after three rings.

"This number is not available!" a monotone female voice announced.

Fuck, he was being screwed over.

He put on a black baseball cap and pulled it low; the rain had been falling slowly for an hour. He opened the door, fully expecting to be rushed by masked men.

He cautiously looked up and down the street, which was deserted. He flashed his key fob at his parked car which flashed three times instead of its normal twice.

He stood tall and cracked his fingers. He told himself he was a survivor from the mean streets of Rathcoole. He had cash, lots of cash. Unfortunately, only Dove knew where it was hidden at the present moment, but he would soon find it.

He strode towards the door and pulled at the handle, which remained firmly closed. He took a step back and again looked up the road before hitting the key fob again. The door locks deactivated, and he jumped inside out of the shower.

The car smelt of new leather and wood. He had picked the car up the day before. It was full of the latest gadgets and gizmos. It was certainly quick enough to run him away from any hit team.

It was a similar activation code which Johnson had electronically grabbed a few hours before as Charlton had made his way back to his car after leaving the local off licence loaded with a bottle of vodka.

"I think that chancer's limp has disappeared, Phil," she commented.

They were parked on the opposite side of Larne Road along a lane which led to Kilroot Energy Park.

He was sitting smiling in the passenger's seat watching for movement on his laptop. He tapped a button and the four-way lights on Charlton's car flashed.

"What are you grinning at, Mr Cheshire cat?"

"Bucking that whore! Where did that come from? You've been watching yourself in the mirror."

"Artistic licence, anyway he's on the move. I'm betting the port to get over to the mainland. His friends in Scotland might protect him."

Johnno's phone rang. It was an unknown number.

"Hello, Phillip, I think you should know that my people have had a confession from those sick bastards that were transporting children across the border and from care homes in West Belfast. We will be making an example of them. Tomorrow's headlines will be about Loyalist paedophiles. The name Charlton and Dove have come up in conversation."

"Thanks, Ma, I appreciate your help. I'm just sorry we couldn't have saved them earlier."

"If you get the morning paper you will also see that the local communities all over the South have risen up and run drug dealers out of the free state."

"Thanks for your help, Ma. I might even bring Bucky over to convalesce when this is all over."

There was chuckling on the end of the line as the phone went dead.

A2 Belfast Road, Whitehead

Charlton had been driving for less than five minutes when she called again.

"Is this the Carrickfergus South East Antrim UVF Brigadier Stephen "Bobby" Charlton, the fuckin' grass? I bet your shit scared in case his story comes out in the 'Sunday World'. Be even worse when they find out about those little kids you've been sending to England." The phone went dead.

"He's took a right on to the Belfast Road, it's a coastal road," he commentated.

"I know this road, it's really tight in places with a drop on the right. It'll be hard to pull him over, Johnno."

Charlton put his foot down as his paranoia grew. The car jumped and slithered over parts of the road as the small drystone wall and the sea below it flashed past his window.

The heat inside the vehicle was growing. He tried to turn down the climate control but to no avail. Then the radio station started to change at rapid intervals. The volume cranked up to deafening levels.

Over a hundred grand he'd paid for this heap of junk. It was doing his head in. In the rear-view mirror, he saw a car in the distance. He couldn't be sure if it was following him, but it added to his growing paranoia.

Ahead was a tight left-hand bend with a lay-by marked with yellow chevrons. A warning sign indicated the need to slow down.

He took a look in the mirror. The car behind him didn't look like a police car and didn't have blue lights or wailing sirens. Relax, he told himself. Probably some old dear on her way to buy the morning groceries.

Johnno looked at the car menu on his laptop. He scrolled down and ticked a box to switch all the vehicle safety features off. He then ticked a box marked 'control'.

Charlton took his foot off the accelerator: it wasn't the cops. He took a deep sigh of relief - which quickly turned to shock as the car began to accelerate.

Desperately he tried to move the steering wheel or change gear, but the car had a mind of its own. He tried the door handle to jump out, but he was trapped.

The car's horn started honking and the four-way flashers and windscreen wipers activated as if the vehicle was possessed.

He took off his seat belt and tried to kick out the windscreen of his remotely piloted car.

He screamed as the car smashed through the stone wall at over a hundred and twenty miles per hour. No airbags came to his rescue as the vehicle nose-dived over the train line and into the jagged rocks below.

The car crumpled, then turned over and sank into the foaming waves.

Loughside, MI5 HQ, Belfast

It had been a very long debrief with senior members of the security services and PSNI hierarchy. The recovered mobile phones from Dove and Sir John Smythe had been a gold mine of intelligence, but not as much as Dove's dozens of pen drives which he had kept, detailing every seedy transaction he had made for both Charlton and Smythe.

Of particular interest was the memory stick marked 'London Account.'

Northern Ireland ballistics services were having a field day with the treasure trove of weapons and ammunition which had been recovered. Of particular interest was a Browning Hi Power pistol stolen from the British army and linked to dozens of murders and punishment shootings and a sniper rifle connected to the shooting of a Protestant family man during a protest march and the murder of Sir John.

Both firearms had Dove's prints all over.

"Oh, and we've just heard that Bobby Charlton has just been killed in a road traffic accident. Seems like he was driving too fast on a very dangerous coastal road and lost control. First reports are that he wasn't even wearing a seat belt," Phos announced.

Clair and Johnno tried to look shocked at the news.

The pair were cross-examined until the only unanswered question was the missing body of Dove. Officers at the scene had confirmed his blood type and DNA were all over the cave.

The amount of blood loss and brain and skull fragments indicated that Dove was dead, but his body had been removed, possibly by his cohorts.

Once the Detectives were happy Mathews ushered Clair and Johnno back to his office.

"Ms Flusk, I have been speaking to your Chief Constable this morning, thanking him for your secondment to this operation."

"Secondment? What secondment was that?" she asked.

"Ever since you started working Mr Johnston, Claire." He shoved an A4 piece of paper across his desk and offered her a pen.

"What's this?" she asked.

"Silence," Johnno told her.

"It's a copy of the Official Secrets Act to ensure nothing gets out. Am I right, Phos?"

John Mathews sat back in his leather chair and placed his hands on the back of his head, smiling.

"Recompense! How did they know, Phos? Little bread crumbs to guide me along the trail, perhaps?"

Phos stood up and looked out of his window towards the garden of remembrance. New flowers and wreaths had been put on the memorials.

"I can neither confirm nor deny the possibility that some form of manipulation has taken place over the last few weeks. What I will say is that everything has been cleaned up and you have contributed to ensuring the safety of UK PLC and the wholesale clear out of the biggest drugs distribution network south of the border."

"Bullshit, Phos, My lads were tethered goats for a lunatic fringe of the Protestant paramilitaries. You knew how I'd react, that I would track them down. Why let them die?"

"I needed you back in the game, Johnno. I couldn't use any assets from over here. You've already identified collusion with the enemy. You were an NOC. Nobody knew you."

"What's an NOC?" she asked.

"Non-Official Cover, working without protection. If we had been caught in the act, we would have been in the shit with no get out of jail free card, with the advantage that we don't have to stick to the rules," Johnno explained.

"Perhaps you should write a book," Phos scoffed.

"What, and die in a dentist's chair? No thanks, Phos. You've bought our silence. Like Mr Dove, it's over. Don't call me for any other little jobs. I take it that the medals are in the post."

They drove away from the tidy white bungalow in silence. Donna had sobbed when he broke the news that Winker had been murdered.

She had even tried to refuse the bags of cash which they insisted she keep as part of her husband's pay out from his last company.

He gave her the address of a good accountant that was very resourceful in turning bundles of dirty notes into clean useable ones.

Claire turned and looked at him closely as he drove back towards her house.

"Well?"

"Well, what?" he asked.

She pursed her lips. "Well, what about us?"

"What about us?" He was showing his poker face.

She punched him hard on his bicep.

"OK, how do you fancy a job on my team over in Manchester? You're a little rough around the edges and I'll have to do some in-depth training with you to get you up to speed, but you might just be good enough."

"I swear, Phillip Johnston, I'm going to fuck you!"

"I really hope so," he grinned.

Private Dining Room, The Jericho Club, London

There were twenty men seated beneath the stunning central chandelier. A grand collection of contemporary art adorned the dark wooden walls.

They were dressed well in dark suits and black ties. The conversation was convivial, pleasant laughter emanated from around the large rectangular table.

All appeared to be well educated, sophisticated, and reputable members of British society. Some were household names, other less recognisable.

A crystal glass was tapped and immediately the conversation died down as the room came to order. At the head of the table the man stood up to address the gathering.

He was much younger than the rest, dark well-cut hair, clean shaven. John Mathews surveyed the room. He knew each and every one of them. He had researched their backgrounds and read every message sent between them on their so-called encrypted phones.

"Members of the Herod Association, welcome to this impromptu dinner - and how fitting you have named your group after the King who ordered the Massacre of the Innocents."

The members began looking around at each other, then at the new man addressing them.

Nobody knew who the new member of their club was. They had all accepted the invitation without question. Jumped into the pre-paid taxis and arrived for the free food and drink. They were all awaiting to be moved again for further entertainment to a more discreet venue.

"How fitting that you all chose to have your last supper at the Jericho Club, the city in which Herod died, after an excruciatingly painful, putrefying illness of an uncertain cause, known to posterity as Herod's Evil."

A grey-haired gentleman at the far end of the table stood up to leave.

"Lord Justice Cooper, if you could return to your seat immediately, please. I haven't finished just yet, Green Seat!"

Cooper looked back in disdain, then opened the door of the private room. Two very large men wearing dark three-piece suits stood guard. Each had an ear piece and the bulges under their left arms indicated that they were carrying firearms.

He looked the men up and down. They didn't smile. Both looked capable and menacing. Cooper turned reluctantly and trudged slowly back to his seat; his legs heavy.

"Thank you, my Lord. Now I must tell you all that your sordid little game is up. My organisation has witness statements, DNA samples and footage of your 'parties' and, suffice to say, you are all looking at substantial custodial sentences."

There was a groan around the room. Mathews noticed some of the perpetrators were crying.

"Who the hell do you think you are, making these false accusations?" a fat red-faced man with a northern accent screamed.

"Sit down, Minister - or should I call you 'Chain and Rampart'? That was your nickname on your EncroChat phone, I believe."

The Minister immediately sat down.

"Gentlemen, of course, to lock you all up will be an expensive trial and the media interest will of course be quite nauseating for UKPLC, so I am offering you an olive branch."

The room went silent as they all sensed an escape.

"You all hold roles of responsibility, you chair and influence high level meetings, some of which are not in the best interest of the establishment. The members of the judiciary here make judgements which are not for the good and betterment of the country. The Lords amongst you block or oppose legislation, so the deal is that you will all start to work for the interests of our nation."

"And if we won't?" the fat MP asked.

"Then perhaps you will be regurgitated by the pigs like the victims you abused."

There was silence in the room.

Mathews took a briefcase from under the table and extracted a wad of A4 sized papers. Each one was a child's photo. He scattered them along the table.

"Look at these poor innocent faces, then come and sign away your very soul."

He pulled out more paper: witness statements to be signed by everyone of the paedophiles. These declarations would be held in secret files only to be used, when necessary, like the sword of Damocles hanging above their heads.

They formed an orderly line and meekly signed the form. There were no disputes or questions, just a blind acceptance that this was the only way to save their skin.

"Let's call this your recompense, Gentleman," Mathews told them.

After leaving The Second Battalion The Royal Regiment of Fusiliers Howard joined Greater Manchester Police as civilian staff member.

His knowledge of covert operational procedures has helped him transition through a number of supporting roles in support of frontline policing.

Fusilier was Howard Lycett's debut into writing and details his twenty-four-year career with the British Army.

Recompense is Howard Lycett's third novel after *Phoenix Dragon* and *Backlash*.

His fourth novel, *97 Hours Looking For War,* is in the process of being written.

Howard is a staunch supporter of Leigh Leopards Rugby League team.

Like his character Phillip "Buster" Johnston he is an avid Jack Reacher fan.

Printed in Great Britain
by Amazon

19975257R00129